STAR WARS
YOUNG JEDI KNIGHTS
JEDI BOUNTY

KEVIN J. ANDERSON
and REBECCA MOESTA

BOULEVARD BOOKS, NEW YORK

STAR WARS: YOUNG JEDI KNIGHTS:
JEDI BOUNTY

A Boulevard Book / published by arrangement with
Lucasfilm Ltd.

PRINTING HISTORY
Boulevard edition / October 1997

The Putnam Berkley World Wide Web site address is
http://www.berkley.com

Make sure to check out *PB Plug*, the science fiction/fantasy newsletter, at
http://www.pbplug.com

ISBN: 1-57297-297-1

BOULEVARD
Boulevard Books are published by The Berkley Publishing Group,
a member of Penguin Putnam Inc.,
200 Madison Avenue, New York, New York 10016.
BOULEVARD and its logo are trademarks
belonging to Berkley Publishing Corporation.

PRINTED IN THE UNITED STATES OF AMERICA

10 9 8 7 6 5 4 3 2 1

To our friend and faithful reader
Deb Ray

acknowledgments

Writing each volume of the Young Jedi Knights requires the help of many different people—Sue Rostoni, Allan Kausch, and Lucy Wilson at Lucasfilm Licensing; Ginjer Buchanan and Jessica Faust at Boulevard Books; Dave Dorman, cover artist extraordinaire; Vonda McIntyre (who created the character Lusa); Mike Stackpole for his help with Evir Derricote and the plague, as well as the Twi'leks; A. C. Crispin for her help with Aryn Dro and Bornan Thul; Lillie E. Mitchell, Catherine Ulatowski, and Angela Kato at WordFire, Inc.; and Jonathan Cowan, our primary test-reader.

JACEN SOLO ADDED another branch to the small campfire. He inhaled the jungle scents that mingled with the spicy smell of burning wood. Yavin 4 was alive and wild and mysterious around them.

His twin sister Jaina stared pensively into the flames, while Tenel Ka, dressed in her usual lizard-hide armor and boots, paced in restless circles around the small clearing. Raynar fidgeted beside Jacen, picking up twigs and tossing them into the embers. His moon-round face had a fretful, haunted look, as if he wasn't at all enjoying their night out camping in the jungle.

Jacen leaned back and lay down with his hands behind his head. Oblivious to the bits of forest debris that distributed themselves through his curly brown hair, he looked up into the star-filled sky and reached out with the Force. He tried to sense small creatures hiding in the jungle around them, but tonight his usual ability eluded him. He sighed. Unfortunately, his Jedi senses picked up mostly his sister's worry, Raynar's anxiety, and Tenel Ka's frustration.

"It's just not the same without Lowie here," Jaina said.

"I should certainly say not," Em Teedee, the miniaturized translating droid, agreed. The little droid hovered with the newfound freedom of the microrepulsorjets he'd had installed on Mechis III. He followed just behind Tenel Ka as she made each restless circuit of the clearing.

Jacen gave up trying to sense small animals. "It's been weeks since Lowie left. He hasn't even tried to contact us." He sat up and looked at his sister. "Hey, you don't suppose Lowie decided to *join* the Diversity Alliance, do you?"

"I hope not. They're the ones who put out a bounty on my father, after all," Raynar answered before Jaina could speak. He clenched one hand around a fistful of twigs until they snapped. "I'll bet there isn't a bounty hunter in the whole sector who's not trying to track down the infamous Bornan Thul and collect the reward Nolaa Tarkona offered." A hint of bitterness infused his words.

Jaina bit her lower lip. Reflections of the flames danced in her brandy-brown eyes. "Zekk's out there with all those bounty hunters—but at least he's on our side. He's taking a pretty big risk, too. If the Diversity Alliance finds out he worked for your father and helped your uncle Tyko, Zekk could be in trouble."

Jacen thought about their dark-haired friend. Zekk had been trained by the Shadow Academy to use the dark side of the Force but had turned away from it. Deciding to start a new life, he'd chosen to become a bounty hunter. With his piercing emerald eyes, excellent fighting skills, and knowledge of the Force, Zekk would be a formidable opponent to anyone who crossed him. "Don't worry about Zekk, Jaina. I have a feeling he can take care of himself. I'm more worried that Lowie might be pressured to stay on Ryloth and work for the Diversity Alliance. You heard what they did to Lusa."

Jaina scowled. "Lowie'd never join a political group that despises humans. He's our friend."

Jacen tried to imagine the lanky Wookiee hating anyone simply because he'd been ordered to. The idea seemed ridiculous. "No, I can't believe he'd go along with that. But why hasn't he at least tried to send us a message?"

"Perhaps he has," Tenel Ka said from the opposite side of the clearing. "He may have been unsuccessful."

Jacen glanced up at the statuesque warrior girl as she broke into a trot. Her red-gold hair, half of which was caught up in Dathomiran warrior braids, flowed out behind her like the tail of a comet.

Em Teedee kept pace with her. "Surely you're not suggesting that poor Master Lowbacca might have been *prevented* from making contact with us!" the translating droid wailed.

"It is possible. If so, he could also have been prevented from returning here," Tenel Ka said.

Jaina groaned. "That would explain a lot—like why the communications center on Ryloth never lets us speak to Lowie when we get a connection through to them."

"Hey, if Lowie's in trouble, then I think we ought to do something about it," Jacen said.

"Agreed," Tenel Ka said, still jogging along the perimeter of the clearing.

Jaina shrugged. "No argument here. If we can't talk to Lowie any other way, we'll go to Ryloth in person."

"Oh my! We could be doomed!" Em Teedee said. "But I *would* gladly sacrifice my last circuit if it would be of any help to Master Lowbacca. Indeed . . . ," the little droid continued bravely, "going to Ryloth may be an excellent opportunity for me to use my translating skills; I *am* fluent in over sixteen forms of communication, you know. Well, I suppose that's all settled, then."

"I guess you should count me in too," Raynar added.

Jacen looked at Raynar. The lightly freckled youth with the spiky blond hair seemed tense and edgy. Raynar's blue eyes followed Tenel Ka and Em Teedee around the circle. Around and around and around. "Do you really *have* to do that, Tenel Ka?" Raynar blurted out at last.

"The jungles are dangerous at night," Tenel Ka replied without slowing. Her voice was steady and she didn't gasp or pant as she spoke. "Tionne advised us to post a watch. Therefore, I am ensuring the safety of our campsite by patrolling its perimeter."

"I knew *that*," Raynar said in exasperation.

Jacen gave a lopsided grin. "We know you offered to take the first watch, Tenel Ka. I think Raynar was just wondering why you're practically running. If you wear yourself out, you'll be too tired to fight against any real threat."

Tenel Ka raised an eyebrow skeptically. "I have found that when I combine physical exercise with my other duties, I am able to think more clearly. It is also an excellent way to release tension."

Jaina chuckled. "In that case, maybe we could all use a good run."

Just as his sister spoke, Jacen sensed it: something out in the jungle watching them. Tenel Ka noticed it too, for she stopped dead in her tracks. Em Teedee narrowly avoided colliding with her shoulder. A split second later the warrior girl dove to the ground and rolled as a snarling, fang-filled ball of fur sprang through the air where she had been standing.

Jacen and Jaina were both on their feet, light-sabers in hand, before the furry creature touched the ground. "It's a rakhmar," Jacen yelled. "Probably looking for a quick meal."

The meter-long beast sprang into the air again, a dynamo of black-swirled fur and snapping teeth. This time, it struck at the only person who had no weapon.

"Raynar, look out!" Jaina cried, leaping after the vicious creature, but Raynar was already moving to dodge the sweeping claws. He launched himself forward, narrowly missing the campfire. Menacing yellow eyes glittered in the firelight. The rakhmar overshot its target and grazed Raynar's leg with its razor-sharp rear claws.

The jungle predator spun around as Raynar snatched a burning branch from the fire, ready to defend himself. The rakhmar crouched on its back legs, muscles coiled, ready to lunge again.

Raynar held his torch high. A strong arm yanked him backward just as the predator sprang—and a pair of lightsabers slashed past him in a parallel glare of emerald green and electric violet. The energy blades sliced the vicious rakhmar into three even pieces that fell to the ground with wet thumps.

With their lightsabers still blazing, Jacen and Jaina inspected the clearing for any other would-be predators.

"I do not believe you will need this," Tenel Ka said, taking the firebrand from Raynar and tossing it back into the campfire. "Your instincts and reactions were commendable."

"Oh, yes. Excellently well done, everyone!" Em Teedee's silver oval floated over to Raynar. "I scarcely had time to be frightened—although I do believe Master Raynar has sustained some injury."

"It's not too bad." Raynar pulled aside his brown Jedi robe to examine the thigh where the rakhmar had clawed it. Dark blood ran from a pair of gashes just below his right hip.

Jaina knelt beside Raynar and examined the leg. "What do you think?" she asked her brother.

Jacen winced. It looked worse than he had expected. "I think we shouldn't have walked all the way here. Maybe we should've borrowed Lowie's T-23 instead. It's a long hike back to the Great Temple."

Tenel Ka pressed her hand against the wounds to slow the bleeding. "Raynar should not walk with this injury," she agreed. "We must bind the leg."

By the light of the campfire, Jaina tore strips of cloth from the bottom of Raynar's Jedi robe. Em Teedee brightened his optical sensors to provide lighting from above while Jaina and Tenel Ka bandaged Raynar's thigh. Unperturbed by all the blood, Tenel Ka wiped her hand on the ground.

"I think I'll be able to walk now," Raynar said bravely, though his voice wavered. When Jacen and Jaina helped him stand, however, all color drained from his face and his knees buckled. Jacen caught him before he fell.

"Dear me! Perhaps Master Raynar would be better advised to rest while one of us returns to the Jedi academy to summon assistance," Em Teedee said. "I believe I would make an appropriate messenger. Therefore, I volunteer to serve in that capacity."

But before the little droid had even finished

speaking, Jacen heard something approaching through the jungle. "We've got company," he said.

Tenel Ka had already assumed a fighting stance, lightsaber drawn, before they identified the sound as hoofbeats.

"Lusa?" Raynar murmured. "Is it Lusa?"

At first Jacen thought his friend must be delirious, but he quickly discovered that Raynar was right. Her rich cinnamon hair and mane flying, Lusa galloped out of the trees. Only when she reached the center of the clearing did she come to an abrupt stop.

In the firelight, sweat glistened on the centaur girl's bare torso and flanks. Her face seemed to go almost as pale as Raynar's when she looked at him. "You're hurt!" she gasped.

Color flooded into Raynar's face. "Yeah, I . . . noticed."

"Hey, how'd you find us?" Jacen asked.

Still looking at Raynar with concern, Lusa answered distractedly. "Before you left Raynar gave me a general idea of where you would be camping. When I got the message, I just headed this direction and hoped to find you."

"Message? What message?" Jaina asked.

"Oh." Lusa stamped a hoof. Her eyes sought out Tenel Ka. "I believe you have a grandmother who used to be queen of the Hapes Cluster?"

"This is a fact," Tenel Ka said.

"Well, she's wreaking havoc with the protective forces stationed in orbit. She asked for Master Skywalker, and when she found out he wasn't here she demanded to see you immediately. Tionne told her that you were out, and the New Republic forces wanted to detain her ship while they ran a background check, but your grandmother wouldn't listen. She must have intimidated the guards somehow, because she'll be at the landing field in half an hour."

Jacen chuckled. "That sounds like Ta'a Chume all right."

Tenel Ka quirked an eyebrow at him. "It would seem we all have business back at the Jedi academy." She turned her cool gray eyes back toward Lusa. "Raynar requires immediate medical attention. He should not walk."

"I . . . I *could* carry him," Lusa said. She sounded rather uncertain.

Jacen knew the idea must have been difficult for the centaur girl. For years the Diversity Alliance had taught her to loathe humans. She was just beginning to unlearn her distaste for physical contact with them.

"I couldn't ask you to—," Raynar began.

"You do not need to ask," Lusa interrupted. She folded her legs to kneel beside him, then spoke gently. "I am . . . offering."

Jacen breathed a sigh of relief.

"Well then," Jaina said, "what are we waiting for?"

It took the companions nearly two hours to get back through the jungles to the Jedi academy. Jaina and Lusa took Raynar into the Great

Temple so that the medical droids could examine him, while Tenel Ka and Jacen headed directly toward the landing field.

An armored Hapan vessel hovered overhead. A couple of New Republic guardian ships had apparently accompanied it down from orbit, and the guards stood awkwardly on the stubbly grass, gazing up at the cruiser.

At Tenel Ka and Jacen's approach, the ship finally descended onto the field. When the exit hatch opened, two dozen armored Hapan soldiers scrambled down the ramp and arrayed themselves around the vessel to form a barrier against anyone who might try to come close to the former Queen of Hapes. Only then did Ta'a Chume herself appear. The aristocratic old woman glided down the ramp, waved an imperious hand to summon her granddaughter and Jacen, and disappeared again into the ship.

Jacen felt nervous as he and Tenel Ka walked toward the ring of guards, who parted to let them pass. The warrior girl led the way into the ship without hesitation.

In the centermost chamber, Ta'a Chume waited for them. She perched regally on a repulsorbench, looking every centimeter the queen that she had once been.

Tenel Ka stopped directly in front of her grandmother. "I assume you have brought information about the Diversity Alliance," she said without preamble.

Ta'a Chume sighed. "Such a beautiful child.

And such a shame about the loss of your arm in that lightsaber accident. If you would only reconsider about that prosthetic limb . . ."

Jacen saw Tenel Ka stiffen. "Grandmother, you did not come to Yavin 4 to discuss my arm."

Jacen was surprised that the former queen did not seem offended by her granddaughter's abrupt answer, and instead merely shrugged and smiled faintly. "No, but you can't blame a grandmother for trying. I did some research for you. . . ."

Tenel Ka nodded. "What have you learned about Nolaa Tarkona?"

Her grandmother's smile grew warmer. "Your instincts about the Diversity Alliance are quite correct. It's more than a simple political movement. The conspiracies and intrigues are almost worthy of the Hapan government."

Tenel Ka scowled. This was not good news. Jacen leaned forward to hear what Ta'a Chume would say next.

"My spies have only begun to uncover a particular truth that the Diversity Alliance hides, even from some of its most dedicated followers. But first, let me warn you: although they preach unity and equality for all alien species, the Alliance itself is as intolerant, in its way, as the Empire ever was. I'd even venture to say that the Diversity Alliance was founded more on hatred of humans than on the ideal of unity."

"Yeah, we kind of got that impression, too," Jacen said.

Tenel Ka's grandmother glanced at him and

continued. "You probably know that the Diversity Alliance's headquarters are on Ryloth, home-world of the Twi'lek race."

Tenel Ka nodded impatiently. "Yes, their leader is a Twi'lek. It was only logical that she would base her headquarters—"

"But what you don't know," Ta'a Chume interrupted, "is that all of the profits from ryll spice—the most lucrative of all Ryloth's exports—have for the past two years been siphoned off to fund the Diversity Alliance."

Jacen listened with interest. His father, Han Solo, had told him about his adventures with glitterstim spice from the planet Kessel, but Jacen knew relatively little about ryll.

"And," Ta'a Chume went on, "those profits have built the Diversity Alliance into a formidable power indeed. The funds have been used to purchase weapons—both legal and illegal—to hire bounty hunters to track down enemies, and to hire assassins to ensure the silence of . . . former friends."

Jacen gave a low whistle.

The erstwhile queen's expression turned frosty. "Apparently, this Nolaa Tarkona is rather more tolerant of her enemies than she is of friends who decide to go their own way. Leaving the Diversity Alliance is a dangerous proposition. *That* is what we have learned so far, but I think we'll find there is much more."

Jacen and Tenel Ka exchanged worried glances.

"Your information is most useful," Tenel Ka

said. "We may need to do further research. Thank you, Grandmother."

"We'd better have a talk with Lusa," Jacen said.

2

RAYNAR WINCED AS the green plasteel medical droid methodically cleaned the gashes on his thigh.

"Is it very painful, Master Raynar?" Em Teedee asked. The little translator bobbed in the air just above the foot of the narrow padded table in the Jedi academy's tiny infirmary.

In spite of the throbbing streaks of fire that shot along his thigh, Raynar didn't want to appear weak in front of Lusa and Jaina. He shook his head. "I'll be just fine now." But he couldn't control his grimace when the medical droid none-too-gently slapped a graft-patch across the deep scratches from the rakhmar.

Lusa gave an impatient stamp with one hoof and moved closer to Raynar. He was suddenly aware that the cool, antiseptic smell of the room had been replaced by a warm scent of woods and spices. He breathed deeply and relaxed a bit.

"Thank you, *I'll* take it from here," Lusa said, shooing away the medical droid. "Jaina, please hand me that anesthetic gel and those bandages."

Raynar watched with detached surprise as the centauriform girl shook back her cinnamon mane and briskly cleansed her hands. With a few quick swipes of anesthetic gel, she deadened the pain in his thigh. Then she began to bandage his leg, her movements deft and practiced.

"You look like you've done this before," Jaina observed, settling onto a stool beside the table.

Lusa shrugged one bare shoulder. "During my time with the Diversity Alliance I became an accomplished medic. Emergencies often arose when we were rescuing the downtrodden. There were many wounds to heal. . . ." She smiled apologetically as she continued winding the bandage around Raynar's thigh. "This is the first time I've helped a human, though." She secured the bandage in place and rested her hand lightly over the wounded area.

"I . . . you do good work," Raynar managed, feeling a sudden feverish heat that had nothing to do with his wounds. "Thank you."

"That's a useful skill," Jaina said. She grinned and winked conspiratorially at Raynar, then looked across the table at Lusa. "I think our patient ought to heal quite well now. Maybe we should ask Uncle Luke about teaching you to use the Force to diagnose—"

Just then the door to the infirmary opened and

a Bothan soldier marched in. The simian-faced alien wore the uniform of the New Republic Forces stationed in orbit around the Jedi academy. His eyes narrowed when he saw Lusa, and his pointed ears twitched.

Em Teedee spun in midair to face the intruder. "I beg your pardon, sir. Might I be of any assistance? Do you have business here in the infirmary, or can I direct you elsewhere?"

The soldier seemed nonplussed and didn't answer immediately. He appeared to be fixated on Lusa. Raynar, who didn't like the way the Bothan was looking at her, propped himself up on one elbow. A sense of foreboding tickled at the back of his mind—or maybe it was just a pang of jealousy. . . .

"Can we help you find someone?" Jaina prompted.

"No," the Bothan said. He took a step forward.

Raynar, feeling unaccountably protective, stretched out his free hand from where he lay and rested it on Lusa's back. Jaina must have been uncomfortable too, he realized, for out of the corner of his eye he saw her hand move to the hilt of her lightsaber. Lusa's back muscles tensed. Raynar threaded his fingers through her mane. He took a deep breath and felt the Force flow through him.

"Hey, how's the patient? All fixed up now?" Jacen asked, trotting through the infirmary door with Tenel Ka beside him. He stopped short when he saw the New Republic soldier and eyed him curiously.

Tenel Ka was instantly on her guard. She arched an eyebrow. "Do you require assistance, sir?"

The Bothan backed up a few steps toward the door. "I—I was told to report to the hangar bay."

"Ah," Tenel Ka said. "Aha. This is not the hangar bay."

"Oh, indeed, sir! Why didn't you say so in the first place?" Em Teedee exclaimed. "I'll escort you there immediately. It just so happens I have business to discuss with one of the astromech units there." The little silvery droid zipped out into the hallway. "It's only one level down. Your confusion is quite understandable, given the amount of reconstruction still in progress here in the Great Temple. If you would be so kind as to follow me?"

With a last reluctant look around the infirmary, the Bothan soldier followed Em Teedee out the door and down the stone walled corridor.

Raynar was about to remark on the strangeness of the encounter when Jacen said, "I'm glad you're still here, Lusa. Would you mind if we asked you a couple of questions about the Diversity Alliance? We have to know."

Lusa, who had just begun to relax now that the guard had left, looked instantly wary again. She took a few steps backward into the corner. "It's important?"

"Very important," Jacen said.

Raynar fixed his attention on Jacen now, hoping that the questions wouldn't upset Lusa too much.

"I need you to promise you won't tell anyone this," Jacen went on, "but we're going to Ryloth. I don't think Lowie knows what you've told us about the Diversity Alliance, and—"

"Who?" Lusa interrupted. She clacked one hoof on the floor. "*Who* is going to Ryloth?"

Jacen made an all-encompassing gesture. "Jaina, Tenel Ka, Em Teedee, and I. Raynar was going to go too, but now that he's wounded—"

"You're not leaving me behind," Raynar objected. "I'll be just fine."

"No! It's too dangerous," Lusa said. "In the Diversity Alliance, hatred for humans is strong. You would be risking your lives to go there."

"What if we pretended to be on diplomatic business?" Jaina suggested.

Lusa shook her head. "They might not dare to harm you in such a case, but they would most certainly turn you away."

"Then we will not enter through the front door," Tenel Ka said. "We will find another way."

"Did you know that the profits from ryll mining on Ryloth are being siphoned off to buy weapons and hire assassins?" Jacen asked Lusa. "We just learned that from Tenel Ka's grandmother."

Lusa's eyebrows rose toward the delicate crystal horns that protruded from her forehead. "The news does not surprise me. I never learned where Nolaa Tarkona got most of her funding. I did know, however, that the Diversity Alliance used bounty hunters and assassins."

"A common enough practice," Tenel Ka interjected.

"We've known for a long time that they used bounty hunters," Raynar said. "They've been trying to capture my father for months."

"But there is more about them that you may not know," Lusa said. "Sometimes Nolaa Tarkona sends assassins to . . . 'deal with' those she believes are traitors to the Diversity Alliance. *Non*humans."

"Well, well, well. I thought Nolaa Tarkona preached that *humans* were the only enemies of the Diversity Alliance," Raynar said.

"True. And that's one good reason none of you should go to Ryloth," Lusa answered. "But there's more. Once, when I had been with the Diversity Alliance for less than a year, a close friend of mine, a Talz, decided to quit. He never told me why he left, though I suspect I now know his reasons. He simply disappeared. A few days later Nolaa Tarkona invited us all to a 'demonstration' in her private grotto chambers."

Lusa's voice grew rough as she spoke, as if she strained against strong emotions. "She gave a great banquet for several of us whom she called her most loyal followers and told us that we would be promoted, given greater honor and responsibility in the Diversity Alliance. Throughout the meal, her Adjutant Advisor Hovrak did not eat. But when we had all finished, Nolaa Tarkona surprised us by having her Gamorrean guards bring in my friend, the Talz. Then, as we all looked on"—she shuddered—"Hovrak made his dinner out of my friend. He killed and ate him right in front of us!"

Jaina gave a wordless cry of disbelief.

Tears trickled from the corners of Lusa's eyes, but she continued speaking as if she did not notice. "While . . . while Hovrak fed, Nolaa gave a speech. 'So it shall be with all traitors to the Diversity Alliance,' she said. She praised us again for our loyalty and ended with these words: 'I believe that the lesson here is simple enough. If you are not a friend to the Diversity Alliance, then you are a friend to our enemies—and a *traitor* to us all.'"

"So it's true," Jacen said. "Lowie may not be able to leave the Diversity Alliance, even if he wants to."

Lusa nodded. "That was one of the reasons I came here with Master Skywalker—because of the security the Jedi academy and its guardian force could offer." She sighed and wrapped her arms around herself, as if the air in the tiny infirmary had suddenly turned icy. Raynar hated to see the tortured look on her face and wished he could comfort her.

"Nolaa Tarkona is very . . . idealistic," Lusa went on. "She believes that all aliens must band together, that only by doing so can they defeat the humans who subjugated them for generation upon generation. If Lowbacca decides to return to his human friends, he will be in danger. He is already trapped."

"But I'm sure Lowie never actually joined the Diversity Alliance. His parents said he only went there to see if he was *interested*," Jaina objected.

Lusa shrugged. "Nolaa might not see it that way. If Lowbacca rejects her beliefs once he understands them, it could be enough for her to brand him a traitor."

"Then we have no choice but to go after him," Jacen said. "We can't leave him in the clutches of the Diversity Alliance."

"This is a fact," Tenel Ka confirmed.

Raynar sat up. "It's all settled, then."

Lusa sighed in resignation. "In that case, you will need my help."

3

NEITHER THE ACHING cold nor the searing heat from the two intemperate halves of Ryloth's surface penetrated to the Diversity Alliance headquarters deep beneath the surface. But in the narrow region where hot met cold, an almost habitable zone of moderate temperature encircled the planet. This strip of mountainous land, only a few kilometers wide, was neither fiery nor frigid, light nor dark, but existed in a perpetual twilight between the extremes. The blast-shielded entrance to Nolaa Tarkona's grotto space dock opened out of a mountainside into this twilight zone.

Lowie couldn't help but be impressed by the variety and quality of ships that passed through the entrance, going about the business of the political movement. Other Twi'lek cities occupied sections of the mountains to the north and south, but Nolaa Tarkona had taken over all the prime areas, including tunnels in and around the main ryll mining centers. Here in Tarkona's headquarters, computer operators, pilots, mechanics, and all manner of workers kept busy night and day.

Lowie's sister Sirra crooned her amazement and complimented the Diversity Alliance on its wonderful fleet of ships. Raaba, who was conducting the tour of the starship grotto, hastened to assure them that not all of the ships belonged to the Diversity Alliance—only the best ones. The remainder were owned by trading partners, diplomats, bounty hunters, political allies, and the occasional mercenary who came looking for work.

Sirra pointed to a clunky, meteor-scarred old vessel clearly used for hauling freight of some sort. The big freighter was just entering the cavernous grotto dock, coughing exhaust and groaning as it extended its landing struts. Sirra joked that the old scow must belong to a garbage trader.

Raaba gave a comradely bark of laughter and leaned closer to her friends. Those battered-looking ships, she explained, came and went regularly. Despite their appearance, on their outward-bound journeys they carried ryll spice ore, a valuable mineral resource belonging to the Diversity Alliance. Though the ryll mined on Ryloth was substantially different in form and potency from the glitterstim spice found on Kessel, it still brought a high price on the open market.

A grin of pride appeared on Raaba's chocolate-furred face. It was part of Nolaa Tarkona's special genius that when she had overthrown the Twi'lek government, she had also taken control of their spice mines. Without the income from ryll, the Diversity Alliance would have had to rely completely on donations from supporters. As it was, credits from the sale of the valuable mineral were used to rescue the downtrodden and to spread the word about unifying all non-human species. The Diversity Alliance would fight for alien rights as no government ever had.

The bulky ore hauler hummed past them and down a side passageway that led to a secured loading area. Half a dozen workers struggled with its cargo containers, while a small traffic-controlling lizard waved brilliant glow-rods to direct the large ships and keep them away from each other.

Although Lowie and Sirra had seen the starship grotto and its various hangar bays before, they had never had a full-fledged tour. Since neither he nor his sister had yet expressed a desire to join the Diversity Alliance, Lowie suspected that Raaba was trying to impress on him the worthiness of Nolaa Tarkona's ambitions.

Raaba probably thought that the flashy new ships and their excellent docking and repair facilities might entice Sirra to join the Diversity Alliance. She was probably right, Lowie thought. But as the tour continued, his own uneasiness did not dwindle. This place, these *attitudes* just did not ring true to him. In fact, the docks only served to remind Lowie that he and Sirra did not have their own ship and could not leave Ryloth whenever they chose. If he asked to go back to Yavin 4, he suspected Raaba would find some excuse to delay him.

Feeling a tingle of his Jedi senses, Lowie turned to find Adjutant Advisor Hovrak watching them intently from one of the small bays. He stood beside Raaba's star skimmer, the *Rising Star,* as if guarding it. Noticing that he had been seen, Hovrak motioned the three friends over.

The wolfman stroked a clawed hand over the *Rising Star*. He suggested that Raaba might want to train Sirra to fly the star skimmer. He advocated that all their members learn everything they could, to reach their fullest potential. Guessing correctly, he said that Sirra had probably never flown such an agile, modern craft before. "Who knows?" the Adjutant Advisor added in a sly voice. "If Sirra proves herself an able pilot and decides to join the Diversity Alliance, I might just need to get her a new star skimmer of her own."

With a sinking sensation in his stomach, Lowie watched Sirra's patchwork-shaved fur bristle in delight as she looked over the ship with shining eyes. She traced her fingers over the *Rising Star*'s hull.

Lowie sighed. He had been hoping to persuade Raaba to take the two of them back to Kashyyyk the next day. He was anxious to continue his Jedi training under Master Skywalker, but somehow he didn't think there was much chance of convincing either of them now. . . .

Without saying anything, Lowie followed after the two young Wookiee women.

He had a very bad feeling about this.

4

THE GRASSY LANDING clearing near the rebuilt Great Temple was damp from an evening shower. Water droplets clung to the lush jungle underbrush that had been pressed down by the frequent shuttles returning from orbit.

The unseasonable rain had been as warm and as brief as a farewell embrace from a friend, but its moisture had brought out all the fragrant exotic scents from the thick forest around them. Everything was quiet, hushed.

The companions worked with quiet speed to make the *Rock Dragon* ready for their unscheduled journey.

Standing outside the *Rock Dragon,* Raynar performed the preflight checks Jaina had assigned him. When Lusa approached, he could sense the centaur girl's presence immediately, as if there were a change in the air temperature. He tried to hurry through his tasks so he could

29

spend a few more minutes with Lusa before they left. At the sound of a hoof impatiently stamping on the soft ground, though, he turned to her with a smile.

In a way, Raynar was glad Lusa wouldn't be coming with them to Ryloth. For one thing, she would be safer on Yavin 4; if the Diversity Alliance captured the centaur girl, it would mean certain death. But also, he couldn't afford to be distracted at a time when he would need all his wits about him to help rescue Lowie. And he found Lusa very distracting indeed.

"I still think you should wait to discuss this with Master Skywalker. He'll be back in a few days," she said, resuming the conversation that had begun hours earlier. "Or at least let Tionne know what you plan to do."

Raynar shook his head. "You know what Jacen and Jaina think. Tionne or Master Skywalker would feel obligated to alert Chief of State Organa Solo. Then it would become a diplomatic incident, and Lowie would become a pawn for the Diversity Alliance. It's better if we slip in ourselves and take care of it quietly, before anyone can get too alarmed."

Lusa tossed back her cinnamon mane. "Well, their mother *should* be told this newest information as soon as possible. Even I didn't know how dangerous the Diversity Alliance was becoming. And *I* was a loyal member for more than two years." Lusa stamped a hoof again to emphasize her point. "Maybe the New Republic should take some action."

Faced with her unaccustomed anger, Raynar was at a loss for words. To his surprise, he sensed that her turmoil was born of concern—and fear—for him.

"If I cannot tell Tionne the truth, what shall I tell her once you are gone? A Jedi would know if I lied," Lusa continued, a storm of deep cinnamon color rising in her face. "And I will not lie, even for you."

Raynar felt a pang of guilt for putting his friend in such a position. He grimaced and rubbed a hand along his aching thigh. At seeing his twinge of pain, Lusa's eyes instantly filled with distress, though they held no less anger. "And *you* are still wounded!" she accused. "You have no business going on such a dangerous mission. You should stay here and recuperate."

Raynar's thoughts churned. The reasons for going to Ryloth had seemed so clear and compelling just a couple of hours ago. How could he stay behind in safety when Lowie's life might be in danger? Then again, if Lusa was correct about the Diversity Alliance, her life could be in danger here, too, no matter what protection the Jedi academy offered.

But what about Raynar's own father? All threats to Bornan Thul's safety had begun on Ryloth. If he could learn anything or find any way to help his father, the key lay in Nolaa Tarkona's headquarters. But if he tried to explain all this to

Lusa, she would protest that being the son of Bornan Thul would only put him in greater peril.

Fortunately, Raynar was spared the need to explain any further when Jacen, Jaina, and Tenel Ka emerged from the *Rock Dragon*.

"Our ship appears to be in excellent condition, Captain," Tenel Ka said.

Jaina grinned. "Checks out perfectly."

"And there are no unexpected creatures as passengers either," Jacen added. "I checked." He looked at the centaur girl. "You're sure you can take care of Nicta and my other pets while we're gone? A hatchling gort needs a lot of attention, you know."

Lusa nodded. "Yes. That will be the easiest part of my duties while you are away."

Raynar cleared his throat. "Um, Lusa wants to know what she should tell Tionne after we leave."

Jaina frowned. "We'll need a few days, at least. You have to stall her that long."

Jacen spoke up. "Hey, I've got a pretty good joke you could tell her."

Jaina rolled her eyes. "Not *now,* Jacen." She looked seriously at Lusa. "I can't ask you to lie, but we do need some time. Once Mom finds out the whole story about the Diversity Alliance—well, as much of it as we know, anyway—she'll do everything she can to protect the New Republic. She might even want to take immediate action."

"And if she did that," Jacen said, "she probably

wouldn't be able to protect Lowie. But he's our friend, and we *have* to do everything we can to get him out first. After that, we'll tell my mother. I promise."

Lusa shook her head, and her diamond horns glinted in the dim light. "I will have to tell Tionne something in the meantime."

"Ah. Aha," Tenel Ka said. "You may tell Tionne this: my grandmother arrived with disturbing news of a conspiracy. The four of us have gone to investigate. This is a fact."

Lusa nodded. "Yes I can tell her that . . . and she will probably assume that you are on Hapes. I don't like it, though. Are you certain you understand the plan we discussed?"

Relief flooded through Raynar. "Thanks for understanding, Lusa. We've got the codes you provided—I think this is going to work."

"Already input the coordinates you gave us," Jaina added.

"Em Teedee's hooked up to the navigational panel and ready to go," Jacen said.

Raynar smiled with more confidence than he felt. "We'll be there and back before you know it."

Lusa shook her cinnamon mane and crossed her arms over her bare midriff. "I doubt that. Do not underestimate the Diversity Alliance."

"Promise me you won't start to worry for at least three days," Raynar said.

Lusa made a noise that was somewhere between a whinny and a snort. "You ask the impossible," she said. "I won't lie. But I will not betray your trust, and I will help you in any way I can."

Raynar reached out impulsively and gave Lusa's hand a grateful squeeze. "I knew we could count on you."

For a moment, Raynar thought the centaur girl would give him a farewell hug; instead, she squeezed his hand in return. Then she reared up, tossing her mane wildly and looking around at the companions. "The plan is a dangerous one," Lusa said. "May the Force protect you." With a swish of her tail, she turned and galloped back toward the Great Temple.

By the time the *Rock Dragon* rose and launched itself into the misty night sky, the landing field was completely deserted.

5

ZEKK TRAVELED ALONE in the *Lightning
Rod*—as usual—searching half the galaxy for
Bornan Thul. As usual.

Through a subspace announcement, the Diversity Alliance had recently increased the bounty
offered for the human merchant, who had been
on the run for months now. Despite the efforts of
the best trackers in the galaxy, Bornan Thul still
eluded capture.

And Nolaa Tarkona was getting quite desperate for the information he carried.

Zekk himself had been face-to-face with the
hunted man. On Borgo Prime, Bornan had hired
him to send a secret message to his family and
also to find his brother Tyko, who had supposedly been kidnapped by the assassin droid IG-88.
But Zekk had discovered that Tyko Thul was in
no danger and had merely concocted a hoax to
lure his brother into the open. But Bornan had
outwitted Tyko and even Zekk.

Zekk still wanted to be the best bounty hunter in the galaxy, yet he could not trust Nolaa Tarkona's motives. Bornan Thul had told him some disturbing things, enough that Zekk knew he could never stomach the consequences of delivering him into the clutches of the Diversity Alliance—no matter how huge a reward she offered.

But few other bounty hunters felt the same moral compunctions.

Now Zekk drifted out in an empty galactic desert between star systems. He had come here following his instincts, not knowing why. As a street-scamp back on Coruscant, Zekk had always been good at finding things . . . and he used those skills now.

The *Lightning Rod*'s sensors were fully alert, tuned in such a way that his entire ship became a listening device, scanning for clues. His computer filtered out trivial hyperwave transmissions, searching for something that would require his attention among the drone of all the other subspace chatter. All directions around him were quiet and still.

He had newly installed scanners and voice identification correlators in his ship, sifters and subject classifiers—the best tracking equipment he could afford. He found it ironic that Bornan Thul himself had made it possible for him to pay for many of the *Lightning Rod*'s upgrades.

After leaving the droid manufacturing world and exposing Tyko Thul's ruse for what it was,

Zekk had found an unmarked deposit in his credit account—payment in full for his services as a bounty hunter. Bornan Thul had been true to his word, and Zekk's obligation to his former employer had ended.

According to the bounty hunter's code of ethics, Zekk was now free to capture the man and bring him in for the reward. Zekk's conscience and his personal sense of ethics, however, would not allow it.

It seemed so unfair to Zekk that the code of honor in his chosen profession would force him to make one decision while his newly regained *personal* honor dictated a completely different course. And then there was his friendship with Jaina, her brother Jacen, and—though he hated to admit it—even Raynar. He could not betray them.

Zekk eased back in his pilot's seat. The dingy cockpit was familiar and felt like home. He liked being alone and self-sufficient, with no one to remember his past. He let his thoughts wander, thinking of Jaina Solo, especially the last time they had said goodbye when he'd left Mechis III.

Jaina wanted badly for him to come back to the Jedi academy, and deep in his heart Zekk wanted the same thing—but he still bore the tremendous guilt of having led the Dark Jedi of the Second Imperium in their attack on Luke Skywalker's Jedi training center. Zekk had been the darkest knight at the Shadow Academy, and he took personal responsibility for all of the death and destruction.

Honor and friendship, Zekk mused. He had given up both when he'd fought for the Shadow Academy. He shook his head.

Never again.

Despite Master Luke Skywalker's assurances, Zekk couldn't just walk back in and believe he would be welcomed without reservations. He had to rebuild his confidence first, to decide in his own mind that he truly wanted to be a Jedi Knight after all. And that he was worthy of trust and friendship.

Still, it would be very nice to be back with Jaina . . . and with Jacen, of course.

Just then one of his numerous sensors triggered an alarm that brought him to full awareness. Thrusting aside all thoughts of Jaina and Yavin 4, he focused his attention down to a laser-sharp point, quickly scanned the control panels, and flicked on the comm system.

The intercepted transmissions were doused with static, warbling and fading as if snatched from a vast distance. The power levels in one of the ships seemed to be rapidly fading. It was a distress signal, but encoded. Why would anyone encrypt a distress signal?

Then he recognized the code—he could not translate it, but he recognized its origin from when he had sent similar signals in the name of Bornan Thul. That was the special encryption used by the Bornaryn fleet!

Zekk knew the identity of the sender even without translating the words. Who else would send a distress beacon directly to the Bornaryn fleet but the man Zekk had seen in disguise on Borgo Prime? The answer was obvious: "Master Wary," who had hired him to go save his brother Tyko.

Now it seemed Bornan Thul was in need of rescue himself.

The second transmission was a gruff warning. "This is Dengar. I claim bounty hunter's right. Bornan Thul is my quarry. I will tolerate no interference."

Previously, Zekk had led Dengar on a merry chase by sending his tracker buoy high out of the galaxy in a fast message pod. The sallow-faced, bandaged human should have gone on a long and fruitless pursuit to nowhere . . . but Dengar apparently hadn't been fooled for long. The cybernetically enhanced bounty hunter thought fast, reacted fast, and proved entirely relentless on the hunt.

He had already found Bornan Thul.

Zekk didn't bother to ponder the bounty hunter's threat. Instead, he punched in coordinates after tracing the signal to its source, powered up his engines, and launched the *Lightning Rod* on a brief hyperspace jump. His instincts had brought him close to Bornan Thul, but not close enough.

Dengar, with his cadaverous face and sunken eyes, had fired upon Zekk without warning on the abandoned ice planet of Ziost. And again, he had destroyed everything in sight on Mechis III—emotionless, relentless, blasting anything in his way.

Zekk's lips formed a thin, cold smile. Dengar needed to be taught a lesson, all right—and he was just the one to do it.

Homing in on the distress signal, Zekk powered up the *Lightning Rod*'s weapons systems. The last time he'd fought Dengar, Jaina had done the shooting while he did the flying. This time Zekk would have to do both. But he still had the advantage, given both his Jedi instincts and the element of surprise.

If he did this right, Dengar would never know what hit him.

He watched the navicomputer, counting down the seconds until he emerged from hyperspace. He kept his hands on the firing controls, intent. In his mind he brought up an image of Dengar's ship, a modified Corellian JumpMaster 5000, imagined its hot engines and every minuscule weak point in its U-shaped configuration.

Zekk cued an ion torpedo as the swirling starlines of hyperspace faded and his ship lurched out into the starfield—and instantly saw the two ships engaged in a dogfight. Dengar's vessel, *Punishing One,* pummeled a crippled and heavily damaged craft that must have been Bornan Thul's.

Even now Dengar's sensors would be sounding an alarm at Zekk's appearance. He had no time to hesitate. Without wasting a heartbeat, Zekk fired his ion torpedo, powered up a second, and launched it.

Both torpedoes flew true—the first exploded beside *Punishing One*'s port stardrive, while his second neutralized the starboard engine.

He opened up the comm channel. "Hello, Dengar—it's me, Zekk. I just wanted to make sure you'd remember who I am."

Dengar's voice, normally gruff and flat, was heated by the fires of outrage. The enhancements to his brain had stripped him of most emotions, but Dengar could still experience rage. "You have broken the Bounty Hunter's Creed. You fired upon me as I pursued another target."

Zekk said, "Your target is also my target, and you're standing between me and my bounty."

Dengar roared. Zekk took careful aim at the *Punishing One*'s communications dish and blasted it to pieces. The bounty hunter could do nothing. His ship hung helpless in space.

Bornan Thul tried to limp away, two of his engines sparking and flaming. Many of the running lights on his ship winked out. Thul's systems were failing.

"Hello, 'Master Wary,'" Zekk transmitted. "We meet again, it seems."

"I should never have been so foolish as to hire you in the first place," Thul said bitterly. "My engines are damaged, my ship in ruins. I don't know how I'll ever make it away from here. I should have guessed no one would answer my distress call but one of you bloodthirsty bounty hunters."

"Actually," Zekk said, "I came to help you get away from Dengar. I . . . I'm not going to take you in."

"Why should I believe you?" Thul shot back. "You bounty hunters are all the same, interested in profit but never in consequences. If Nolaa Tarkona gets the information I have, the whole galaxy will become a charnel house."

"You mean the navicomputer Fonterrat gave you?" Zekk asked, gambling with what he already knew.

"Fonterrat? What do you know about him? That sniveling worm would let billions die for his own profit."

"Fonterrat is dead—as are all the people on the human colony of Gammalin. It was a plague." Zekk had been to the modest settlement, wiped out down to the last inhabitant by a horrible disease unwittingly carried there by Fonterrat, a small-time scavenger who had made the mistake of doing business with Nolaa Tarkona.

Bornan Thul groaned. "Perhaps it is too late then."

"*What's* too late? I can help you protect the information you have—"

"No one can help me," Thul said flatly. "Especially not a bounty hunter."

"Listen, I found your brother Tyko, didn't I?" Zekk said. "I've spent time with your son Raynar. Why won't you trust me?"

"I can't trust anyone," Thul said. "There's too much at stake. The Diversity Alliance has infiltrated everywhere. I can't even be sure of the New Republic. The Alliance has spies in the military, in the government."

Thul's ship staggered away, as if running at only 10 percent power. Zekk couldn't believe the man was still trying to escape when he had so little chance. The *Lightning Rod* could run him down in an instant.

In his pilot's seat, Zekk felt a sudden chill of warning down his spine. His rear sensors showed Dengar's ship powering up again, its lights flaring, weapons systems coming to bear.

"What?" Zekk exclaimed. The blasts of his ion torpedoes should have knocked the *Punishing One* out of commission for hours—but Dengar must have been prepared for such contingencies. Maybe he had repaired his communications quickly as well, Zekk thought. "Dengar, behave yourself—or do you want me to shoot you again?"

In response, the other hunter fired three precisely targeted turbolaser blasts at him. Reacting immediately with his Jedi instincts, Zekk spun the *Lightning Rod* about in a corkscrew trajectory that took him up and away from the line of fire.

Intent only on escape, Bornan Thul continued to limp away in his damaged craft, gathering speed, trying to change coordinates to where he could escape into hyperspace.

"Oh no you don't," Zekk said, and took off after

Thul. He saw the hyperdrive engines glowing on the fugitive's battered ship. Somehow Thul had gathered the power and speed necessary to escape. He must be making his computations right now!

Zekk toggled up a special torpedo, aimed carefully at the sluggish ship, then launched it. The torpedo sailed across space, a pinprick of fire that hit the hull of Thul's craft an instant before the ship blurred, elongated, and then snapped away, streaking through into hyperspace.

One of Dengar's engines flickered to life and he fired again at Zekk. The wounded U-shaped craft picked up speed, pursuing with murderous intent.

With a flash, another ship emerged from hyperspace, and Zekk recognized the odd shape of Boba Fett's *Slave IV*. Fett streaked into the fray, entering with all weapons primed. In a moment this place would be crawling with greedy bounty hunters who had picked up Thul's distress signals. They were like predatory fish chasing after wounded prey.

Zekk decided the best thing to do right now was to get away, so that he could track down Bornan Thul in his own time.

He had chosen a very narrow and dangerous course. The trackers were a rough bunch, unruly and deadly, and they only operated according to certain terms. Zekk had violated those terms. He had taken sides against most of the other hunters. And Bornan Thul didn't even believe his motives.

But Zekk knew that bringing in Raynar's father could prove deadly for humanity. He had been to Gammalin. He had seen how the virulent disease had swept through the population. Was Bornan Thul a carrier of the plague? What information did Fonterrat's old navicomputer contain, and why did Nolaa Tarkona want it so badly?

Dengar's recovering ship rounded on the *Lightning Rod* and opened fire. Zekk again dodged as he punched coordinates into his navicomputer.

From *Slave IV* Boba Fett also issued a warning, ordering Zekk not to flee. Zekk knew he could not possibly escape from the combined efforts of Dengar and Boba Fett.

Leaving the dueling field behind, he flew off, closing his mind to the shouts of outrage that poured from his comm system.

"Sorry, Fett," Zekk muttered under his breath. "I know you won't understand, but it was the only way I could live with myself." Dengar's and Boba Fett's words cut off abruptly as soon as he launched into hyperspace.

Relaxing slightly, Zekk permitted himself a slow sigh of relief and pleasure. He was confident now that his position was clear.

And all was not lost. Yes, Bornan Thul had escaped . . . but Zekk had borrowed a trick from Dengar.

Just in case Thul wouldn't listen to him—as had indeed proved to be the case—Zekk had prepared a tracking device, a torpedo carrying a transmitter that would strike and cling to the fugitive's ship.

The transmitter would activate in a couple of days, and then Zekk could find Bornan Thul anytime he wanted. It would be as easy as following the blips. . . .

But finding the hunted man was one thing—figuring out how to help him was quite another.

6

AS THEY APPROACHED the Twi'lek home-world, Jaina maintained sufficient distance that the *Rock Dragon* would appear as an indistinguishable blip against the stellar background. The fire and ice planet hung tantalizingly close, but Jaina did not dare move nearer. The Diversity Alliance was extremely watchful.

"Finding Ryloth's the easy part," she said, turning slightly in the pilot's chair. "Getting *into* Nolaa Tarkona's tunnels is going to be the real trick."

The Twi'lek clans had built their homes by boring into cliffsides and creating enormous cities, complete with towering structures, in caverns and grottoes that were protected from the harsh environment of the planet's surface. Nolaa Tarkona had taken over a prime section of tunnels not far from the ryll mining areas, and the Diversity Alliance now controlled Ryloth and held its population in an iron grip.

"We must be patient," Tenel Ka said. "Lusa was certain that the correct opportunity would arise. The plan should work."

"Excuse me, Mistress Jaina," Em Teedee piped up from where he had been wired to the navigational console, "my initial scans indicate substantial traffic in the vicinity of Ryloth. The planet appears to have many orbiting vessels as well as frequent arrivals and departures of automated industrial ships in the inhabited sections of the mountains."

"*Industrial* ships?" Jacen said. "What kind of industries do they have on Ryloth—other than mining, I mean?"

"Actually, mining ryll spice *is* Ryloth's major industry now." Raynar seemed glad to show off his knowledge of interstellar commerce. "Ryll is a rare mineral with medicinal uses. It's fairly valuable, and it was used during the Krytos plague when the Rebels took Coruscant. Of course, before Nolaa Tarkona took over the government, a good part of Ryloth's income came from a huge black-market slave trade in dancing girls, administrators, accountants, and so on. The trade still exists, but now it's more secret than ever. Twi'leks are famous for doing business behind the scenes. They usually slink and hide and work in shadows to pull their strings. Nolaa Tarkona, on the other hand, doesn't seem to keep a very low profile."

"Ah. Aha," Tenel Ka said. "Ryll is now Ryloth's

major export, and Nolaa Tarkona siphons away profits to fund the Diversity Alliance."

"Probably practices a bit of piracy to build up her resources," Jaina added. "Gets the rest in donations from her converts."

"Converts like Lowie," Jacen said, and a feeling of gloom passed over the young Jedi Knights. "We've got to find him and rescue him."

The companions waited for hours, using Jedi relaxation techniques with varying degrees of success. Their ship hung motionless in space, a bit of insignificant galactic flotsam, unimportant, unnoticed.

Finally, a sensor blip caught Jaina's attention, and she leaned forward. "Large craft coming into the system, approaching on our vector." She backtracked its path. "Looks like an empty drone of some sort."

"It appears to be on autopilot, Mistress Jaina," Em Teedee confirmed.

Raynar leaned closer to peer at the sensors. "Good. It's one of those automated ore haulers Lusa told us about. You know—the ones that come to Ryloth, pick up raw ryll material, then take it off-planet for processing."

"Then this is the one we'll use for camouflage," Jaina said, biting her lower lip. "It's big enough. Shouldn't be hard to hide in its shadow."

"This is a fact," Tenel Ka agreed, "but the Diversity Alliance will be vigilant."

"Sure. Lusa warned us about that," Jacen said,

scratching his tousled brown hair. "We'll just have to be extra careful."

"A commendable philosophy, Master Jacen," Em Teedee agreed.

As the lumbering ore hauler continued toward the planet, its uneven shape filled much of the starfield in the viewports. Jaina skillfully maneuvered the *Rock Dragon* behind the giant robotic craft where its bulk would eclipse their own ship.

"Now we'll just slip in and no one will notice," she said with a bit more confidence than she actually felt.

Jacen's brandy-brown eyes squinted as he studied the pitted surface and blocky configuration of the ship that would serve as their shield. "Looks like it's seen better days."

The ore hauler was a giant rust bucket that looked as if it had served as a freighter since the Clone Wars. Its outer plating was scored from cosmic radiation, solar flares, and a few potshots taken by space pirates. The bulk of its body consisted of tetrahedral storage bins linked together in a hodgepodge cluster. Some of the storage bins had broken latches; others looked as if they had been welded shut.

Raynar leaned forward and whistled. "In my parents' fleet, we overhaul all the hull plating long before it can pick up that much ionization damage."

Propulsion systems lined the rear of the hauler, glowing white. A computer-guided bridge console lay buried deep within the ship's core like the rudimentary brain of a prehistoric creature. Jaina noted no weapon emplacements—no defensive systems whatsoever, in fact.

She nudged the *Rock Dragon*'s repulsorjets, tweaking them closer and adjusting her speed to match the hauler's exactly. "We're just going to hitch a ride here," Jaina said. "Hang on while I get closer."

"Dear me, this may require some rather difficult flying, Mistress Jaina," Em Teedee said. "Please allow me to assist you with the coordinates."

She looked over at the empty seat where Lowie usually sat. "All right. I could use a little help from a qualified copilot at the moment."

The little droid's sensors dimmed as he frantically ran calculations on the navigational computer.

Biting her lower lip, Jaina dusted her fingers across the guidance controls and eased the *Rock Dragon* closer and closer to the corroded hull. She adjusted their speed minutely, moving to place the Hapan passenger cruiser exactly on top of one of the tetrahedral cargo containers.

With a *thunk,* the ships joined, and Jaina engaged a magnetic locking device that would fix the *Rock Dragon* in place. She let out a sigh of relief and sat back, crossing her arms in satisfaction. "There! That ought to do it. Now we can ride the ore hauler right on down. They'll take us along as part of the package . . . and we'll slip into Nolaa Tarkona's tunnels without any trouble at all."

Heavy blast doors groaned open on the mountainside, exposing the starship grotto in the caves of the Diversity Alliance. On schedule, the ancient ore hauler followed the automated beam to its cleared landing area. With a burst of repulsorlifts and a backwash of dust and exhaust fumes, the clumsy freighter settled to the rock floor as workers scrambled to receive it. They prepared for another important shipment offplanet.

Computer engineers logged the hauler's arrival and more loads of ryll ore were sent up from the deep underground mines. A hodgepodge group of Diversity Alliance recruits and recommissioned droids waited for the safety lights to wink off on the hauler's guidance console. Gamorrean guards watched the activity, marching back and forth to look busy.

The business of the Diversity Alliance had to proceed without delay—and Adjutant Advisor Hovrak made sure there were no complications. The proud wolfman stood clad in his clean uniform, proudly watching the activity around him. The spray of medals and ribbons on his chest gleamed.

"Prepare for work," Hovrak said with a growl. "We have to fill this ore shipment and send the transport away. The processing facility is not yet operating to its full capacity, and the next vessel is already approaching orbit. Now, move!"

"Yes, sir," a Gand said, his voice puffing beneath his respirator mask. He moved slowly, punching a request into an electronic pad at his side. From other catacombs came heavy, metal-sided carts filled with ryll-rich rubble that had been mined by the slaves down in the deep tunnels. The Gand directed a work crew to attend to the arriving carts.

Hovrak gazed at the automated freighter, which reminded him of a bantha sleeping in the desert sun. Its sides creaked as it adjusted to the extreme temperature variations, freezing in space and burning through a steep descent in the atmosphere. Everything checked out.

This old robotic craft had been donated to the Diversity Alliance by a Hig trader. Occasionally, the alien captain flew a run or two herself, but most of the time she let automated pilots take care of the drudgery while she remained on a backwater world enjoying herself at a cantina.

As other recruits rushed about to take care of exporting the next shipment, Hovrak clasped his clawed hands behind his back. Full of his responsibilities for Nolaa Tarkona, he maintained a rigidly upright posture and marched on an inspection tour around the ore hauler.

He scrutinized the front cargo pods, the large metal-walled bays, the rear propulsion systems. The battered ship was much the worse for wear, but the Diversity Alliance couldn't be choosy . . .

and this ore hauler had served Nolaa Tarkona well.

Soon, when humans were gone from the galaxy, the other alien races would share in a great deal of wealth, Hovrak mused. For now, though, they would have to bide their time, waiting until Nolaa's plans came to fruition.

As he rounded to the port side of the ancient hauler, though, Hovrak's daydreams were interrupted. He came to an abrupt halt as he saw a small craft attached to the side of one of the tetrahedral cargo bays. An intruder! Someone had slipped through the Diversity Alliance's orbital defenses!

Hovrak shouted to sound the alarm. Docking-bay workers poked their heads out to see the cause of the commotion. The wolfman marched around the grotto, shouting for guards.

Corrsk, the Trandoshan killer, as well as four more Gamorrean guards charged into the starship grotto. The guards drew their weapons, in search of something to shoot. With a bulky scaled paw, Corrsk knocked them aside, wanting to score the kill himself.

Hovrak roared, and the security forces came around to the back of the automated ore hauler. The wolfman stood tall to glower at the unexpected ship attached to the hull. "That's a passenger cruiser," he said, and sniffed the air. "A Hapan design, I believe. I want to get to the bottom of this."

Corrsk looked suspicious, narrowing his huge

slitted eyes. "Prepare your weapons," he growled at the guards.

Hovrak marched over to an access ladder and climbed up to where the strange craft clung to the ore hauler. It had been magnetically attached. "Let's get inside," he said, then stood back, not wanting to get his uniform dirty.

The Trandoshan pushed his way forward and found the access hatch. He worked the priority override designed into the airlock, and the Hapan cruiser opened with a hiss as the pressures equalized. Cold, stale air rich with human scent filled Hovrak's nostrils. Bristling with anger, he sniffed, and sniffed again as he crawled inside. The other guards drew their blasters as they dropped down into the pilot compartment, then marched toward the back passenger seats.

But they found no one. The ship was empty.

Hovrak went to the cockpit console and called up the data he could find. The rest was encrypted. "This ship is called *Rock Dragon,* a small passenger cruiser . . . abandoned, it seems. Sent to us for salvage." He curled back his lips to bare his fangs.

The Trandoshan poked through the ship, his nostrils flaring. "I smell humans," he said. "Kill humans."

But though Hovrak and the Gamorreans and Corrsk scoured the small passenger cruiser, they found no secret compartments—and no sign of any human passengers.

"Very well," Hovrak said, "we'll consider it a

gift. Arrange to have the ship removed to the small-craft bay. We can put it to use." He climbed out of the hatch, then bellowed down to the other workers. "Go get the ryll cargo containers! We need to bring the ore up and get this ship launched again."

The Gamorreans and Corrsk stalked across the grotto toward the small-craft bay, where they could fetch a mechanic to disconnect the *Rock Dragon* and pilot the cruiser to safe storage.

Hovrak leaped down and went to report. Nolaa Tarkona ought to know about this ship. Perhaps she'd have some suggestions on how best to use it.

As he left the starship grotto, Hovrak saw the Trandoshan standing at the edge of the grotto. Corrsk sniffed the air again, looking around suspiciously. Then he departed, leaving the *Rock Dragon* unattended and alone.

The cargo hatch of one of the tetrahedral holding bays cracked open just enough for a silvery ovoid to lift up on its microrepulsorjets. Em Teedee rose above the edge of the cargo hauler, then performed a pirouette. His optical sensors glowed as he scanned the grotto.

"I see no one, Mistress Jaina. It seems we're in the clear."

"If we are clear," Tenel Ka said, unseen in the storage bin, "we must move quickly."

The cargo hatch popped entirely open. Jacen and Jaina scrambled out to stand on the stained hull of the ore hauler. They shucked their flexible environment suits and stowed their helmets and suits back in a corner of the storage container.

"Good thing we hid in here," Jacen said, noting the open hatch of the Hapan passenger cruiser. "I'll bet they gave the *Rock Dragon* a pretty thorough search."

Raynar clambered out, flushed and panting. He brushed wrinkles from his drab Jedi jumpsuit. "I don't think Nolaa Tarkona is gullible enough to believe that story about finding the ship in space," he said. "We should get far away from here before they come back to make a more complete search."

"Too late," Jaina said. They heard the thunder of machinery and the sound of approaching feet marching from deep underground catacombs. "They're going to get the ore hauler prepped and ready to launch again."

The young Jedi scampered across the stone floor of the starship grotto and ducked into a dimly lit side tunnel. Em Teedee bobbed along behind them on his repulsors.

"Well, we did it," Jacen whispered, turning around to clap a congratulatory hand on Tenel Ka's shoulder. "We're here. Now all we have to do is find Lowie."

"Yes," she said. "And now our danger is greater than ever. We are in the lair of the Diversity Alliance, and if they capture us we may not escape with our lives."

7

NOLAA TARKONA STRODE through the carved rock corridors, brooking no delays as she descended toward the small-craft bay. The *Rock Dragon* awaited, and she wanted to see it with her own rose-quartz eyes. Dark robes that hid most of her body swirled around her as she walked. Everyone who caught sight of her determined expression hurried to get out of her way.

Hovrak kept pace beside her, his uniform trim and free of stains. The wolfman took special care to protect the clothing from blood spatters during his violent meals. It was just one of the ways in which he expressed his pride at being her Adjutant Advisor.

"This way, Esteemed Tarkona," he said. "I've chosen one of our Sullustan mechanics to fly the ship to where we can give it a thorough inspection."

"Yes . . . be very thorough." She frowned.

"Something about the convenient appearance of this craft makes me uneasy."

Without turning, Nolaa scanned the tunnels behind her with the optical sensors embedded in the stump of her severed head-tail. It always paid to remain vigilant for spies or assassins. In the grotto light, her tattooed head-tail twitched, indicating her agitated state.

Nolaa was not nearly as attractive as her half sister Oola, but she had developed *power* instead of grace. Nolaa had learned to manipulate people. She achieved her ends through inspired rhetoric. Her half sister had died because of her beauty, kidnapped by the vile traitor Bib Fortuna and sold to Jabba the Hutt, who had killed her on a whim and fed her to the horrible rancor.

Nolaa had a much more important destiny, though. She would hold the future of entire worlds in her clawed hands. And *she* would bring about the end of the human race.

She and Hovrak emerged into the rocky chamber of the small-craft bay. With a whine of low-power engines the *Rock Dragon* floated in from the nearby starship grotto. Despite a few uncertain stutters and overcompensations at the helm, the pilot seemed to know what he was doing. Nolaa admired the skill of the large-eyed, mousy alien in the cockpit who maneuvered the Hapan craft into the open area of the low-ceilinged chamber. The other spectators stepped back to give Nolaa room.

The passenger cruiser bore a few exterior

markings, mostly ornamental . . . but no serial number or special designation. Either its original owners didn't care about such legal trivialities, she reflected, or they had something to hide.

"A nice ship to add to our collection," Nolaa said. "Unfortunately, it won't augment the military branch of our fleet."

Hovrak rubbed his claws together. "But the Diversity Alliance cannot depend on military might alone, Esteemed Tarkona. Though we have the moral high road, we do not have the strength of numbers; it is possible we never will. We must win the battle through other means."

"Our time is running out!" Nolaa snapped. She clenched her jagged teeth, which she had recently filed sharp again. "That is why we *must* obtain the plague! Where is Bornan Thul?"

She scowled, staring toward the heavy blast doors that sealed the opening to the small-craft bay in the cliffside. "I am astonished at that human's resourcefulness. He should have been captured and brought to me months ago." Her hand squeezed into a fist so tight that her pointed claws drove into the skin of her palm, drawing dark blood.

"We've raised the bounty," Hovrak said. "Soon Fonterrat's navicomputer will be in our possession, and we can find the Emperor's plague storehouse."

Nolaa shook her head, her tattooed head-tail swaying from side to side. "We've already offered enough credits to interest everyone with any talent. We need a lucky break. We need someone to come across the right clue."

She focused her pale eyes on the *Rock Dragon* as the Sullustan pilot set the craft down and shut off the repulsorlifts. She scowled again and turned to Hovrak. "Run a full data check on this vessel. I want to know everything about it." Her face held a troubled expression. "It probably has nothing to do with Bornan Thul, of course. The ship is of Hapan design, and the Hapans are not allied with the Bornaryn fleet—at least we don't think so."

The Sullustan pilot popped his head out of the *Rock Dragon*'s hatch and jabbered something about how well the passenger cruiser handled. He bowed respectfully to Nolaa before Hovrak shooed him away.

The Trandoshan representative entered the landing bay, stamping his feet. Corrsk sniffed, scanned the area with his orange eyes, rippled the armored scales on his hide. His muscles bunched and he crushed his wide jaw together with displeasure, sampling the air. He eyed the *Rock Dragon* with instinctive loathing, then went directly to Nolaa Tarkona.

"You seem agitated, Corrsk," she said. "What are your concerns?"

Corrsk inhaled deeply and shook his massive head. "Smell Wookiee. Trandoshan hate Wookiee." He glared at the *Rock Dragon*. "Human ship. Should be no Wookiee there."

Nolaa remembered that earlier in the day

Raabakyysh, Lowbacca, and Sirrakuk had worked on ships in the small-craft bay, tinkering with engine systems and sharing maintenance suggestions. All of their jobs had been tracked by the headquarters' exhaustive computerized record systems. The residual scent of Wookiee fur must still be hanging in the air, Nolaa thought, though she herself could not detect it.

"Make peace with your primal desires, Corrsk," Nolaa said, her voice firm but understanding. "I know Wookiees are your natural enemies, but in the Diversity Alliance we rise above such things. We have one true enemy: the New Republic, the humans . . . those who would deny us our rights as sentient beings. Don't waste your time on the wrong target."

"Kill humans?" Corrsk said. "Haven't killed any humans *yet*." He drew in a snarling, hissing breath.

Nolaa nodded in commiseration. "I sympathize. I can't wait until we are finally able to obliterate their despised race—but for that to happen, the Diversity Alliance must work together. If the Empire and the Rebels could call a temporary truce at Bakura, then we must show ourselves superior to them. We can have a lasting peace among alien species."

The Trandoshan nodded, and his wide shoulders sagged with the difficulty of the task she had set for him.

"Your anger is a good thing, Corrsk—if you know how to use it properly."

The Trandoshan drifted away, still uneasy. He remained suspicious, but Nolaa did not question him. Perhaps the scaly predator would find some detail they needed to know. She decided it would be best to leave him alone.

Nolaa turned to Hovrak. "Get to work on identifying that ship and its history," she said. "Keep me apprised of your progress."

After Hovrak bowed low, clenching his clawed hands, he rushed off down a corridor to his work. Several other tunnels and transport trains led to the deep excavation mines, ore shipment centers, and terminus rails. Nolaa glanced at each tunnel, studied the activity in the small-craft bay for a moment, then headed back toward her own private chambers, where she could think, where she could feel safe.

Humans had committed so many crimes against alien species throughout history, she thought bitterly. Even though these tunnels were her place of power, Nolaa Tarkona did not feel absolutely protected anywhere. And the mystery of this unoccupied Hapan ship made her far more nervous than she could allow Hovrak or Corrsk to see.

When she returned to her throne room grotto, Nolaa intended to relax and let waves of contemplation sweep over her. She wanted to sit back under the brilliant scarlet banners of the Diversity Alliance and think of her overall plan, how her group could achieve its magnificent goals. Her visions of the future inspired her.

But before she had relaxed for even two minutes, a Duros communications specialist swept into her room. The alien's sunken, noseless face and blue skin, his squared-off head and wide, pupilless eyes, gave him the appearance of a mummy. He moved very quickly, as if agitated.

The Duros bowed perfunctorily and said in a watery voice, "Esteemed Tarkona, you have a message from the bounty hunter Boba Fett. He wishes to speak privately with you."

Nolaa was startled. The masked bounty hunter would not call unless he had something important to tell her. She hoped the news was good, but she feared his message was something she would not want to hear.

Nolaa went into her isolated office, stood by the polished black table, and activated the inset holoscreen. Fett's helmeted head appeared. He nodded slightly as he spoke, but she could see no other indication that anything human or alive hid beneath the slitted Mandalorian visor.

"Nolaa Tarkona," he said, "two of us found Bornan Thul."

Her heart leaped, but Fett's voice did not carry a gloating or triumphant tone. "He escaped us— but not without assistance, and only temporarily. I am confident I will bring him to you before long."

"You communicate with me simply to report *failure*?" Nolaa demanded. "I'm beginning to believe, Boba Fett, that your reputation is undeserved."

"It is deserved well enough," Fett said. His voice remained neutral, as if he was incapable of taking offense. "Thul has proved to be considerably more skillful than I had anticipated—but I enjoy the challenge."

"Why did you call, then?" Nolaa asked. "I am very busy."

"To inform you of a new enemy, a bounty hunter who helped Thul escape. Either Dengar or I would have secured the item you seek, had it not been for this traitor's meddling."

"Who?" Nolaa demanded. "Who is this traitor?"

"His name is Zekk," Fett said. "The young man seemed naive. He claimed to be in training as a bounty hunter. But he turned against us and Bornan Thul slipped away."

Nolaa Tarkona seethed. Everything seemed to fall apart and become complicated, when it should have been so simple! Without even answering, she severed the transmission link. She clamped her mouth shut and allowed the anger to boil within her. New enemies cropped up everywhere, and the Diversity Alliance's battle grew more and more difficult each day.

But this fury did not drain her; it tempered her, adding endurance. She had told Corrsk that his anger was a good thing if directed at the proper target—and Nolaa Tarkona had many targets indeed.

Corrsk climbed into the impounded *Rock Dragon*. His scaled feet clomped on the deck plates. He moved about, sniffing, touching seats, opening storage lockers. With his clawed fingers he ripped open one of the rear passenger chairs, but found no hidden weapons, no clue as to the ship's origins.

The ship's computer had apparently been coded with unbreakable passwords, though Corrsk suspected that the Diversity Alliance's expert slicers could dig out all the information he needed. They would rip the answers from the *Rock Dragon*'s memory banks.

The stench of humans was strong, heating his blood, increasing his desire to kill. Everything around him took on a reddish tinge as his stalking lust increased. His claws flexed like durasteel talons; his muscles pumped like the pistons of an Imperial walker.

He had waited too long to fight—waited too long to kill. He *needed* to find a victim soon or he would go into a murderous frenzy and slaughter everything in sight.

Corrsk inspected the *Rock Dragon* again, searching for any shred of evidence. Then, focusing on his olfactory senses, he returned to the copilot's chair and inhaled deeply. A familiar scent, delicious . . . and infuriating.

He hadn't been certain before, but now he knew that he detected more than just the pungent, overpowering smell of human. . . . Mingled with it was the incredible, distinct aroma of Wookiee. But not just any Wookiee. This was the unmistakable scent of the ginger-furred one Nolaa

Tarkona had welcomed into the Diversity Alliance, the one Raaba had recruited and brought to Ryloth.

Lowbacca.

He smelled Lowbacca, here in the impounded ship. The lanky Wookiee had some connection with this mysterious passenger craft.

The Trandoshan growled deep within his throat. He sensed a deadly plot here: danger and betrayal. Lowbacca must have something to do with the *Rock Dragon*. What treachery was he planning?

Corrsk growled again as he climbed back out of the small ship. He would keep this information to himself for now. He would have to be content in the knowledge that the time for bloodshed would be soon. Very soon.

He would get his chance to kill humans. And at least one Wookiee . . .

8

TENEL KA LED the way through the dim and winding tunnels, her warrior senses alert, every muscle taut and ready. She was acutely aware of the danger they faced: anyone who noticed the companions would immediately recognize them as intruders in the realm of the Diversity Alliance. Nolaa Tarkona would not tolerate the presence of humans.

Jacen clung close beside the warrior girl, and together they used their Jedi senses, casting out through the Force like a net for any glimmer of their friend Lowbacca.

Raynar struggled to keep up with Jaina, who hung back a bit, staying close to him in case he needed her help. He limped a little on his healing leg, but made no complaint. The little translator droid hovered between them at shoulder level, bobbing along as part of the expedition.

With whispering footsteps as quiet as spring

leaves brushing together, the young Jedi Knights hurried down one long corridor to an intersection. Tenel Ka paused, studied the adjacent corridors, and listened. Finally, detecting a slight tingle of Lowie's presence, she chose a corridor that led in that general direction. "This way."

She touched her rancor-tooth lightsaber, fingering the carvings on its hilt. "If we are seen," Tenel Ka said, "we should return to the *Rock Dragon*. We must use our lightsabers—the fight will be for our very lives."

"I propose that we not allow ourselves to be seen in the first place," Em Teedee said. "It would be entirely too dangerous."

"Great suggestion," Jacen said, rolling his eyes. "Now why didn't *we* think of that?"

They saw alcoves chopped out of the rock walls, and passages that plunged steeply down into deeper rock. The entire mountainous region of Ryloth was a tangled warren dug out by the Twi'leks over thousands of years. Many of the tunnels were now unused, the sites of battles in ancient clan wars.

In her training as a princess of Hapes, Tenel Ka had learned about many distinctive civilizations, including the Twi'leks. Short on resources and living space, the Twi'lek culture had developed into a violent and angry one. They had built several underground cities of linked caverns and tunnels, cramped hives for the various clan factions. Since the Twi'leks could not easily spread out into the inhospitable territory of the frozen night side or the burning day side, they were forced either to dig new tunnels or to kill each other off and keep their population to a manageable level.

Nolaa had chosen isolated tunnels far from the cavern cities for her headquarters. From there she could direct space traffic and ryll mining operations. In her takeover she had disposed of the leaders of the most powerful clans. Now she controlled the planet through the ostensibly noble and peaceful rule of the Diversity Alliance—not to mention a carefully chosen assassination here or there when it became absolutely unavoidable.

Tenel Ka crept forward, using all senses: touch, sight, hearing, smell . . . and the Force. The air tasted of damp coolness and rock dust with a sour undertone of moss and fungus, and the faint metallic odor of minerals and old blood.

Tenel Ka motioned for the others to follow her as she hurried through an uncomfortably long stretch of corridor. She normally enjoyed running at full speed, but here she felt naked and exposed. Some guard might see them and sound the alarm at any moment. But she heard no movement, no footsteps, only a trickle of water that ran from a crack in the ceiling above.

Tenel Ka chose another dim tunnel and turned left. She had just turned again into a side passage when she heard the clomping of something large around a blind corner ahead. In fact, several somethings—or some*ones*.

Jacen brought himself to a skidding halt, and she pushed him back the way they had come. The young Jedi Knights scrambled for cover.

"In here, quick!" Jaina whispered, pointing to a small storage alcove. "We've got to hide."

A tarpaulin just large enough to conceal them hung across the opening. A bright blue triangle had been painted on the rock beside the opening; Tenel Ka did not recognize the symbol, but this was no time to speculate about what it might mean. Jaina drew the tarpaulin aside and tugged Raynar into the alcove. "What are you waiting for?"

They ducked inside, and Em Teedee barely managed to zip beneath the thick cloth before it dropped back into place. The four sat crouched in the shadows, holding their breath, listening intently. Raynar looked pale and frightened, but ready to fight if necessary. Jaina sat next to him, wearing a grim expression. Though the caves were cool, Tenel Ka could feel perspiration trickling down her back beneath her scant reptile armor.

With a clank and a shuffle, three hulking guards rounded the corner. Their heavy footsteps pounded closer, accompanied by grunts and snuffling sounds.

Around the edge of the tarpaulin, Tenel Ka saw three squat Gamorrean guards stride by on patrol. The huge brutes seemed wary, their piggish eyes open for any intruders. The guard on the right stumbled and lurched into the one in the middle, who shoved him back. The Gamorreans snorted at each other, then continued plodding along.

Tenel Ka narrowed her granite-gray eyes and heaved a faint sigh of relief after the guards moved past the hidden alcove.

Jacen touched Tenel Ka's arm and indicated the storeroom where they had taken refuge. "Hey, look at this," he whispered.

"Oh my!" Em Teedee brightened his optical sensors to help light up the shelves. "I daresay this is quite an impressive array of firepower!"

All around them, shelves were piled high with blasters and laser rifles, thermal detonators and sonic grenades. The weapons were stacked haphazardly, stockpiled by the Diversity Alliance—just in case they should ever need them for an ultimate battle against their human enemies, no doubt.

Tenel Ka felt cold. Nolaa Tarkona was ready for an all-out war against the New Republic, even if she didn't capture Bornan Thul.

Now, it was more important than ever that they escape—not just to get their friend Lowbacca to safety, but also to warn the New Republic about the enormity of the impending threat.

Tenel Ka considered taking weapons with them, but blasters and grenades weren't the weapons of a Jedi. She believed she and her friends could get in and out without having to fight. She did, however, make a mental note of the blue triangle symbol that marked the arsenal's location, just in case they were forced to fight their way back out.

The four companions slipped back into the corridor. They checked the tarpaulin to be sure it hung naturally, as it had before their arrival. Then Tenel Ka and Jacen cast out with their minds again. The glimmer of the Wookiee's presence seemed brighter now.

"That way?" Jacen said, pointing.

Tenel Ka nodded. "Come," she said, creeping along a sloping downhill path. "We must find Lowbacca and leave again before it is too late."

Raaba's chocolate-brown fur bristled with pride as she led Sirrakuk down to the small-craft bay, where personal ships belonging to the Diversity Alliance were reconditioned, upgraded, and sent out on missions.

Sirra wanted to take a look at the strange new vessel that had arrived attached to a robotic ore hauler. Raaba was happy to provide her with the access clearances. She felt great pleasure that her young Wookiee friend enjoyed the new things she had seen in the Diversity Alliance.

Lowbacca, on the other hand, seemed moody and distant, and Raaba was afraid she hadn't managed to convince him of the logic in Nolaa Tarkona's arguments. She couldn't understand what was wrong with him, why he couldn't see clear reason; if nothing else, his emotions should have persuaded him when he heard the heart-breaking tales of human cruelty to alien species!

But he had spent his last few years being brain-washed by humans. Raaba had her work cut out for her.

Today Adjutant Advisor Hovrak had taken Lowie down to the main computer center and assigned him the task of optimizing the inventory programming. While working with the computers, the lanky Wookiee had appeared somewhat happier, his mind preoccupied. That, Raaba thought, was at least a step in the right direction. . . .

She and Sirra entered the small-craft bay. Raaba's skimmer, the *Rising Star*, was in a reserved berth near the huge bay doors, ready for her to take off whenever she wished.

At the moment, though, Raaba's highest priority was to ensure that Sirra and Lowie adapted well to the Diversity Alliance. The Twi'lek leader had made it clear how valuable she considered the new Wookiee recruits, particularly Lowbacca with his Jedi abilities. Raaba would not let her leader down.

Sirra stood in the bay, her eyes as bright as new credit chips when she saw the vehicles arrayed under the lights. She had shaved additional decorations on her shoulders and arms, and now the patches of hairless skin stood out in interesting contrast to her thick fur. She wore the unusual look at the wrists, neck, and ankles with a greater verve and imagination than she had before. Tufts of fur stood out in odd patchworks and curled designs.

Not satisfied with working in the computer factories like her parents, Lowie's sister had undergone training on Kashyyyk to become a starship pilot. Sirra had dreams of her own, and Raaba intended to play on them. The Diversity Alliance could fulfill those dreams as the New Republic could not. Sirra let out a yip of delight when she saw the mysterious salvaged ship.

Two Ugnaught mechanics briskly scoured the hull seams, cleaning away the carbon scoring and polishing up the old passenger cruiser. Sirra studied the craft, noting the lines and the Hapan design.

Raaba, though, froze as she recognized the *Rock Dragon*. She had seen this ship on Kuar, flown by Lowbacca and his friends—his *human* friends! What was it doing here?

Her dark nostrils flared as she sucked in a deep breath. Something was terribly wrong. Raaba looked around the echoing cave chamber, past its bustling mechanics. Her eyes narrowed as she scanned the numerous tunnels where humans could hide. Spies? She unconsciously pushed her armbands tighter against her biceps. Human spies, creeping around in the private sanctuary of the Diversity Alliance!

Oblivious to Raaba's tension, Sirra leaned forward to study the ship; she seemed eager to sit behind its controls. Raaba gestured for her to do as she wished, and Lowie's sister sprinted toward the open passenger cruiser. With absolute fascination, she investigated the engines, the hull, the landing struts, before finally clambering inside.

Raaba held back, feeling her stomach knot. What if Lowie's friends had come to abduct him, to steal him away from his place in the Diversity Alliance? It would be a decidedly human thing to do. Humans were sore losers, she thought, unwilling to let aliens make their own choices.

Raaba hurried over to a communications console, switched to a private channel, and summoned Adjutant Advisor Hovrak. In the growling Wookiee language she rapidly told the angry wolfman of her suspicions.

Hovrak snarled. "I knew there was something strange about that ship," he said. "I must increase security. Raaba, join me in the main grotto, and we will send out search parties from there. Is Lowbacca still stationed in the computer center?"

She nodded, and Hovrak said, "Good, then we will concentrate our search in that area. If we can keep your friend distracted, perhaps he will not realize anything is happening. We can take care of this before it becomes a problem."

Raaba clenched her powerful fists and her biceps bulged against her armbands. Lowie. The young Jedi Knights were undoubtedly looking for him.

Jaina led the way next, her senses tingling. "Lowie's close," she said. "He's just up here."

"Be careful, Jaina," Tenel Ka said.

"I'm careful," she answered. Jaina paused at the corner to detect any alien Diversity Alliance soldiers in the next section of tunnel, but it too was empty. Eerily quiet. They had been incredibly lucky so far.

These catacombs seemed abandoned. When Nolaa Tarkona took control, she had slaughtered many Twi'leks who fought against her—and now this section of tunnels was indeed like a tomb.

The floor grew smoother, as if heavy footsteps had polished the rough-hewn stone. Ahead, Jaina saw several corridors that branched around the same central place, a large room with glassed-in walls and a support structure holding it up; heavy-duty recirculation fans fed in cooling air. Computers and terminals filled the enclosed chamber—and there, flanked by a Sullustan and two polished hacker droids, sat Lowie!

"There he is!" Jaina said in a hoarse whisper.

"I'm certain he'll be most pleased to see us," Em Teedee said at her shoulder. "I simply do not know how he manages to get by without me."

The ginger-furred Wookiee hunched over a terminal linked to a mainframe. His lanky arms hung down as he studied a screen, deep in concentration. He punched buttons on a keypad. Symbols scrolled up past his eyes. Lowie nodded, then moved to a different terminal.

Before anyone could stop her, Jaina hurried out into the tunnel intersection. She would have to get Lowie's attention, but it seemed impossible without also sounding an alarm.

Em Teedee swiveled in the air, his optical sensors glowing. "I'm certainly anxious to speak with Master Lowbacca again."

Not wanting to be left behind, Raynar and Jacen accompanied Jaina, scurrying forward, keeping low. Tenel Ka hesitated, looking around in the dim tunnels instead of ahead. "We must be cautious." Then she felt a cold shiver of warning up her spine.

Jaina spun around, also sensing it, just as Em Teedee let out a thin wail. "Oh dear, they've found us."

Tenel Ka whirled to face a large group of one-eyed Abyssin armed with spiked clubs, a towering Trandoshan reptile, and a wolfman who appeared to be the leader. He grinned with triumph, showing off his fangs.

Tenel Ka grabbed for her lightsaber, but the alien soldiers already had their blasters drawn. The wolfman barked a quiet order. "No lightsabers, Jedi Knights," he said, "or we will cut you down where you stand. I am Hovrak, and every soldier here obeys my orders."

An Abyssin reached up to snatch Em Teedee out of the air.

"Let me go, you brute! Be careful—you'll scratch my casing."

"No outbursts, no noise," Hovrak warned. "You will come with us quietly."

From another tunnel a second group of soldiers emerged. With them stood Raaba, chocolate fur bristling, red headband cinched around her head, and armlets pushed high on her biceps.

Jacen looked desperately at the Wookiee woman. His eyes pleaded. "Hey, Raaba, tell them who we are! We just wanted to talk to Lowie."

But the plea was wasted. Raaba glared at them.

In a smooth motion their captors swept them into a side catacomb, away from the computer center. Jaina drew a deep breath to shout for Lowie—but the Trandoshan clapped a rough reptilian hand across her mouth.

"Kill humans," he gargled, as if in anticipation.

The monsters hauled the young Jedi Knights off as prisoners. The guards remained wary, keeping their blasters pressed against their sides. The companions could never coordinate their Jedi powers all at the same time to divert so many blaster bolts.

Jaina swallowed hard. They would fight to escape—but now was not the time. . . .

Back in the computer center, Lowie sensed a great uneasiness in the Force. He looked up from a difficult problem at his terminal, glanced around the computer center, and then darted his gaze out through the transparisteel walls into the shadowy corridors beyond.

Although the interior light caused quite a glare, and he could make out only a few details, he thought he saw a flicker of shadows, a movement of bodies disappearing into a corridor . . . but he could not be sure.

Once again he felt the heavy loneliness he had almost forgotten during his deep concentration. He loved working with computers, and this programming problem was a great challenge. He stared out the windows for a long moment, but nothing reappeared. Then with a low sigh he sat back down at the keyboard and returned to work.

It was probably just his imagination. Lowie missed his friends terribly, and he must have been seeing only what he wanted to see.

9

STRUGGLING IN HOVRAK'S grip, his wrists tied behind him, Jacen cast about in his mind for some way of using his Jedi abilities to free himself. The wolfman's claws dug through the sleeve of his flightsuit, piercing his skin and drawing a few sticky droplets of blood. Jacen barely felt the pain, though.

He looked over at his sister, then at Tenel Ka, to reassure himself that they were all right. The warrior girl showed no sign of agitation, but when her granite-gray eyes flicked toward him, he saw grave concern. He drew a deep breath and called on the Force for the calm courage he needed, to keep up a good face for her. The Diversity Alliance attackers didn't deserve the satisfaction of seeing their fear.

The other young Jedi Knights remained silent as Hovrak and the guards marched them through an endless maze of corridors until they finally emerged into Nolaa Tarkona's throne room grotto. The Twi'lek woman sat stiffly in her stone chair on the dais, leaning forward. Her glittering pink eyes intent, she watched them with barely disguised loathing.

Jacen stared back at the scarred leader of the Diversity Alliance. Her skin was pale and cadaverous, and the masculine uniform and padded body armor Nolaa wore beneath her flowing black robe hid any feminine curves she might possess. Even so, she radiated power as she watched the young human captives.

"Ah, a gift for me," Nolaa Tarkona said. "Or perhaps a snack for Hovrak."

Hovrak's hot breath blew down Jacen's neck.

"We're not a gift for anyone," Jaina snapped. "Or a snack."

Nolaa's tattooed head-tail twitched. She displayed a set of perfectly pointed teeth. "You are trespassers—intruders, spies. Worst of all, you are *human*." She spat the word and scowled with distaste. "Humans have always tried to destroy what alien species have built. This is my private sanctuary, a place of freedom for all species. Still you have crept in and contaminated this place with your presence. You were caught near the computer center, no doubt attempting sabotage."

"No way!" Jacen said. "We only wanted to see our friend Lowbacca." He struggled in Hovrak's grip and looked over at Raaba, pointing at her with his elbow. "Raaba knows. We're friends of Lowie's. We just need to talk to him."

The chocolate-furred Wookiee woman took this as her cue to march toward Nolaa Tarkona with the three lightsabers the soldiers had confiscated, as well as the silver translating droid, which had been powered down for storage.

Nolaa looked at the Jedi weapons and then up at Raaba. "You know these humans? How so?"

Raaba averted her eyes, flashed a venomous look at Jacen for having embarrassed her, then growled an answer. Even with Em Teedee switched off, Jacen could understand many of her words. Raaba explained that these were Jedi trainees from Master Skywalker's academy on Yavin 4. They were former companions of Lowbacca's, but now that Lowie was with the Diversity Alliance, Raaba was certain he knew who his true friends were.

"This is a fact," Tenel Ka said. "And *we* are his true friends. For this we do not need to tell him lies, as you do."

Hovrak lashed out to cuff Tenel Ka, backhanding her with a hairy paw. She reeled at the blow, but did not cry out in pain.

Jacen struggled backward, hoping to kick Hovrak, but to no avail. Then he calmed himself. He was a Jedi, he reminded himself. He would use the Jedi way. Letting his eyes fall half shut, he reached out with the Force and detached all fourteen of the glittering medals Hovrak so proudly displayed on his precious uniform.

To the wolfman's surprise, the emblems sprang away from his shirt to scatter jingling on the floor. The Adjutant Advisor roared and bent down to grab the medals, but they leapt from his hands and fell tinkling to the rock floor again.

"They must die," he said, glaring at the companions.

"Eat them," the Trandoshan heartily agreed. "Kill humans."

Standing beside Nolaa Tarkona, though, Raaba glanced sidelong at the young Jedi Knights. She seemed uneasy, and Jacen wondered if perhaps the Wookiee woman felt guilty about what she had done.

Raaba took a step closer to Nolaa's stone chair. In a low voice, she argued against the Adjutant Advisor's brutal suggestion, insisting that the young Jedi Knights were too important to be killed. Their deaths could cause significant problems for the Diversity Alliance . . . but if the need arose, they could fetch a fine ransom or be used as hostages. The Solo twins were the children of the New Republic's Chief of State. The warrior girl was a princess of the powerful Hapes Cluster.

Raaba hesitated, then looked at young Raynar as a growl built in her throat. Her words to Nolaa were so husky and quiet that Jacen had to strain to hear them. And this young man, she told her leader, was the son of *Bornan Thul*.

The Twi'lek woman's face lit up with delight. "Bornan Thul is your father?" She ran her tongue along the sharpened points of her teeth.

Raynar flinched and took a step back.

"You'll never find him," he said. "Whatever it is you want from my father, you won't get it."

"Perhaps we won't *need* to find him, if we've found you," Nolaa said, favoring him with her broadest smile. "And children of the Chief of State, daughter of the House of Hapes—you may serve us well indeed when the Diversity Alliance launches its all-out war against humanity."

Nolaa's dark robes flowed around her, obscuring her padded armor, as she stood up. Her tattooed head-tail twitched, and all of the Diversity Alliance soldiers came to attention, sensing their leader's agitation.

Hovrak still scrambled around on the stone floor, picking up his scattered medals, growling in frustration. He hadn't quite comprehended yet that Jacen was the cause of his embarrassing clumsiness.

Standing calm and motionless, Jacen fixed his attention on the three deactivated lightsabers lying unattended on the dais. He focused his mind on his own weapon, then on Jaina's, then on Tenel Ka's. He knew how they worked, knew how to manipulate them.

Nolaa Tarkona clenched her clawed hands at her sides. Her eyes were like two bright lasers. Her head-tail twitched.

Her feet were very near the lightsaber handles.

Jacen reached out with his mind . . . and with a *push* he pressed all three power studs. An emerald-green blade, an electric-violet one, and then a turquoise one sprang out like spears toward Nolaa Tarkona's feet.

She reacted with astonishing speed, leaping back. The lightsabers writhed as if they were alive, or possessed. The handles vibrated with power, but so far only the hem of Nolaa's black robe was slashed and singed.

The guards bellowed at each other, causing an uproar. The Gamorreans appeared confused by this new development. Hovrak bounced to his feet, dropping all of his medals again.

"Jedi powers," Nolaa said. "They're using Force tricks!"

The Trandoshan hammered Jaina to her knees. One of the Abyssin knocked Tenel Ka aside.

Raynar shouted, "Leave them alone!"

Raaba hurried forward and carefully but frantically tried to grab the handles of the lightsabers to protect Nolaa Tarkona. One of the guards hurried forward, afraid of the Jedi blades, but knowing he had to do something.

"Kill the human Jedi," Hovrak snarled. "All of them. It is the only way to prevent such incidents."

The alien guards brought up their blasters, targeting the young captives. The Diversity Alliance soldiers were clearly ready to follow the Adjutant Advisor's orders without question.

Jacen stepped forward. "No, wait! We surrender." He used the Force again, struggling hard to maintain sufficient concentration—and switched all the lightsabers back off.

The guards looked down at the three handles as if they were unpredictable poisonous snakes. Raaba reached forward and gathered them up with a growl.

"Do not kill the humans yet," Nolaa Tarkona said, breathing heavily to control her anger. "These four are too valuable, and we must plan accordingly." She fixed them each with an ice-pick stare. "However, I think it would be best if they were to disappear for now."

"Wait. Please let us talk to Lowie first," Jacen said. "Just for a few minutes."

Nolaa pursed her lips in mock regret. "Sadly, Lowbacca must never know of your presence here," she said. Raaba crossed her arms firmly over her chest and nodded vigorously. She seemed to understand that her present tenuous friendship with Lowie would be damaged if he knew his human friends had come to rescue him—and that Raaba had prevented them from seeing him.

"Lowbacca remains with us," Nolaa said. "And you, too, will serve the Diversity Alliance. After all the pain and loss humans have visited upon alien species, it is only fitting that you now work to profit the Diversity Alliance. Consider it a form of atonement." She gestured toward one of the side corridors. "Take them down with the other slaves. They will work in the ryll caverns until we decide how best to use them . . . or until the work itself kills them."

The young Jedi Knights struggled as the guards dragged them away from the throne room, but Jacen knew there would be no escape from the spice mines of Ryloth.

10

NOWHERE.

For the moment, Zekk had decided to go *nowhere*. After his brief encounter with Bornan Thul and the other two bounty hunters, Zekk had made a short hyperspace jump to the vicinity of a small and unremarkable star system. He let the *Lightning Rod* drift in the laser-sharp blackness of space. The dwarf star itself was the only bright spot of light anywhere near.

Zekk had no appointments, no known destination . . . and he needed time to think.

For now, this was the perfect spot. No distracting planets or spaceports, no ship traffic. No fields of asteroids littered the area about him. No gaseous anomalies or nebulas lit the darkness with their multicolored glows.

Even the *Lightning Rod* seemed strangely silent in its operation, as if it were holding its breath to give Zekk time for peaceful introspection. He welcomed the solitude, since he had a great deal to think through. Nothing was clear at the moment.

Dimming the lights inside the cockpit, Zekk leaned back in the pilot's seat to organize his thoughts.

He was satisfied for now with what he had accomplished by planting a tracer on Bornan Thul's ship. Zekk had been careful to ensure that the remote wouldn't put Thul at risk. He had set its automated transmitter for delayed activation, to keep other bounty hunters from picking up and identifying the signal before Thul left the area. Also, if Bornan Thul himself became suspicious of the "dud" torpedo and ran an immediate check on his own ship, he would detect nothing. It would be a full two days before the tracer beacon would activate.

That was time enough for Zekk to figure out some way to make Bornan Thul trust him. But he knew it might not be very easy. From what Thul had said, he trusted no one with the "information" he possessed. Zekk shook his head in irritation. Didn't Thul realize that holding the information back, that trying to keep it a *secret,* was more dangerous than simply sharing what he knew with the New Republic?

But what could Thul possibly know that Nolaa Tarkona wanted so desperately? And what kind of knowledge would Bornan Thul hide from *both* the Diversity Alliance and the New Republic? Zekk tried hard to piece together what he knew.

Clearly, this whole situation made sense to No-laa Tarkona and to Bornan Thul. Unfortunately, neither of them had been generous enough to let Zekk in on the secret. Between what he had learned from Fonterrat's message cube, recorded just before the scavenger had died on the ill-fated colony Gammalin, and what Bornan Thul had let slip during Zekk's conversations with him, there had to be an answer.

As his ship slowly rotated in the emptiness, a bright streak curved across the unrelenting blackness of space, just a few hundred kilometers in front of the *Lightning Rod*. A comet, Zekk realized, its long ghostly tail evaporated by the distant warmth of the small sun. Intrigued, he decided to follow the glowing ball of ice that trailed a ribbon of sparkling vapor behind it.

Zekk watched it for a moment, then set a course in his navicomputer so that the *Lightning Rod* would parallel the beautiful comet and keep pace with it on its long, slow journey around this solar system. He grimaced at the irony: despite the technology Zekk had at his disposal, the comet seemed to have a stronger sense of direction than he did. The evaporating ice ball sailed confidently along on its course, needing no one to direct it, no navicomputer to guide it or make course corrections—only the pull of gravity.

A frown wrinkled Zekk's forehead as he tried to recall something that Fonterrat had mentioned about the navicomputer. Bornan Thul had claimed to have "information" that could put millions of lives at risk. Human lives. Immediately after his secret meeting with Fonterrat on the isolated world of Kuar, Thul had decided to disappear.

Fonterrat had mentioned giving Thul a navicomputer module. And it seemed that the navicomputer was the one thing Nolaa Tarkona desperately wanted. But what information could it hold? The location of something? What had Nolaa lost . . . or what did she need to find?

Because Nolaa had loosed the plague on Gammalin, Fonterrat had expressed his hope that the Diversity Alliance would never find Bornan Thul and his cargo. Could there be a connection, then, between the navicomputer and the *plague*?

The plague *had* killed every human on the colony, but then it had died out. Surely Nolaa Tarkona could make no further use of it.

But if Nolaa ever found the original source of the plague, it was possible that nothing would ever stop the spread of the disease.

Zekk shifted uncomfortably at the thought. Fonterrat had said something about giving Nolaa Tarkona two samples. Surely one more vial could do no worse than the first had— though that was bad enough. But what if Nolaa decided to unleash the plague on Coruscant, for example? Or what if she found a way to replicate it, and infect all human worlds?

No. Fonterrat had seemed fairly certain that this was not possible; otherwise Bornan Thul could never have thwarted Nolaa Tarkona's plan just by hiding from her. What then, would the *navicomputer* tell her?

Something clicked in Zekk's head. It was almost like one of those puzzles that Jaina's younger brother Anakin loved to solve. Suddenly, a dozen snatches of conversation and stray bits of messages whirled together and resolved themselves into a logical pattern in his mind. Without understanding for certain how, he *knew* now what Bornan Thul had.

Fonterrat's navicomputer must contain the location of the place where the scavenger had found the plague. The two small samples must have been Fonterrat's bargaining tools, samples to show his good faith so that the Diversity Alliance would barter with him for more. But Fonterrat had not trusted Nolaa Tarkona enough—with good reason—to sell her the information directly. And in the end, something had caused Fonterrat to warn Bornan Thul about the danger he carried.

The scavenger had clearly wanted to profit from the information, but maybe he had hoped the Diversity Alliance would never use it. Nolaa, however, *had* used the sample he had given her. Indiscriminately.

Yes, it was possible, Zekk thought. But where could such a horrible plague have come from? A planet with no human population? Somewhere in the Outer Rim? But surely a planet with a virus so deadly to humans would have been reported long ago.

Or the disease could be some substance that had been found by a mining company in an asteroid or a comet. It was even possible that some crazed alien on an uncharted world had actually *developed* the virus on purpose.

In any case, Zekk knew he'd have to gain Bornan Thul's confidence, if he was to be of any help to the man. Thul couldn't protect such an important secret forever. Zekk would be able to find him as soon as the homing beacon activated. And if he managed to get a lead on Bornan Thul, it wouldn't be long before one of the other bounty hunters was successful as well . . . someone sly and skillful like Boba Fett.

Still staring at the glowing streak of comet in front of him, Zekk shook his head. He couldn't allow that to happen. If anyone could get Bornan Thul to trust him at this point, it would be his son Raynar.

Zekk set his mouth in a grim line. He hoped Raynar would believe him when he explained the urgency of the situation. Zekk thought he had established a basis for trust with Raynar on Mechis III, but he'd have to convince the young man once and for all that he no longer wished to collect the bounty on his father.

Zekk now knew exactly where he wanted to go. It was time to pay a visit to Yavin 4. With growing anticipation, he leaned forward and entered a new set of coordinates into his navi-computer.

Zekk turned the *Lighting Rod* in a quick arc and peeled away toward the Jedi academy, leaving the comet to streak onward alone in the darkness.

11

TENEL KA WATCHED one of the Gamorrean guards shove Raynar, who fell hard against the mine car that would take them deeper underground. "I'm cooperating—there's no need to get rough!" the young man objected. He regained his balance and stumbled onto the prisoner transport vehicle.

When the guard muttered something vaguely conciliatory, two other Gamorreans cuffed their apologetic companion.

In silence the young Jedi Knights climbed aboard the mine car and eased themselves onto the dirty metal seats. The guards held tight to handles beside their seats as the vehicle accelerated with a lurch. The mine car picked up speed, carrying them farther from Nolaa Tarkona's throne room, farther from their impounded ship . . . and farther from Lowie.

Staring out the open sides of the vehicle, Tenel

Ka watched the walls blur by. She noticed places where chunks of rock had broken away, as well as scars and craters left by blaster fire that had ricocheted off the stone. Much of the fighting during Nolaa's revolution must have taken place down here, when the old Twi'lek clans had fallen to the reactionary Diversity Alliance.

When the vehicle stopped, the companions were ordered to get off. Though they all stood immediately, Hovrak grabbed Tenel Ka by the arm and yanked hard. "Stop gawking at the walls, human—you've got work to do."

Tenel Ka's poise was good, and she managed to keep her balance. Even so, Hovrak's sharp claws scratched her unprotected skin. Warm blood flowed from a shallow wound on her upper arm, but she refused to give him the satisfaction of seeing her wince in pain.

"Hey, leave her alone!" Jacen said, trying to push his way forward.

Hovrak dismissed the tousle-haired young man with a snort, then looked pointedly at the stump of Tenel Ka's other arm. "You are lucky the Esteemed Tarkona considers you too important to kill. You are sure to be a burden down in the spice mines. We won't get much work out of a one-armed female. Worthless."

Tenel Ka reacted with spring-loaded reflexes, whirling about to slam the flat of her hand full force against Hovrak's snout. The impact made a sound like ripe fruit struck with a hammer. Continuing her spin, Tenel Ka brought her booted foot up and kicked the wolfman unmercifully in the abdomen. Then she lashed out with her other foot to smash him sharply in the knee.

Hovrak fell.

It all happened in two seconds. The Adjutant Advisor yowled in unexpected pain even before the blood began to spurt from his smashed snout. The other Jedi Knights could not leap to her aid before Hovrak's guards dragged Tenel Ka away from him—but she was finished.

One eyebrow arched, the warrior girl shot Hovrak a look of challenge. "Perhaps a one-armed female is not quite as helpless as a complacent wolfman," she said coldly.

Hovrak coughed blood and got back to his feet while the guards chuckled at her retort. They froze, looking sheepish, when Hovrak glared at them. Struggling to regain his dignity, he wiped a sleeve of his uniform across his snout. Blood smeared the meticulously clean cloth.

"Throw them in with the other mine slaves. And if this girl's production is one gram less than the requirement . . . we shall see how well she can work with *no arms*."

Many Twi'lek caves began as natural formations that were hollowed out over centuries of labor into a larger and larger underground labyrinth. As the civilization expanded and the population grew, they dug deeper into the mountain ranges.

By accident the Twi'lek people had discovered

veins of the precious mineral ryll, a form that was sometimes called spice. Ryll had numerous uses—medicinal and otherwise—and the Twi'leks immediately became important suppliers, often working with smuggler lords and contraband shippers.

Small cracks and tunnels in the living rock had been expanded by slaves into echoing chambers until the mines grew huge and unsupported. Finally the walls had collapsed—freeing new veins of ore at the expense of the poor, crushed workers. Their Twi'lek masters had not deemed this expense unreasonable.

As Tenel Ka and her friends were led into the mines, she let her gray eyes adjust to the harsh, uneven light. The majority of labor parties she saw around them consisted of human prisoners. Apparently proud, Hovrak pointedly explained to his new workers, "Those slaves are pilots and smugglers that crossed Nolaa Tarkona, not to mention a few hapless captives taken from small craft we found in nearby systems. If anybody noticed their disappearance, it would have been dismissed as a mere space accident. Now, working for the Diversity Alliance gives meaning to their pitiful lives."

A few of the downtrodden miners were Twi'leks who looked emaciated and beaten. Tenel Ka watched them with interest, recognizing that these must have been outcasts or survivors from the Twi'lek clans Nolaa had squashed during her takeover of the government. The lucky ones, it seemed, had died during the fighting.

To illuminate the ryll excavations, the slave masters had brought in wide glowpanels powered by self-contained generators. The portable units shed their garish light onto the main work areas. The stark contrast between this high-powered brilliance and the shadows in the walls, corners, and jagged ceiling hurt Tenel Ka's eyes.

Clusters of strange, lumpy fungus grew from crevices in the walls like melted, foaming plastic. The pale fungus oozed a sickly, sweetish odor that turned her stomach.

The ceiling itself was a festival of stalactites, with spiky banners unfurled and stabbing down toward the floor. Her sharp eyesight showed Tenel Ka that the stalactites were the same strange fungus. The white, foamy mounds seemed to grow and pulse in the bright illumination from the glowpanels.

Dust and sweat and fear mingled with the sickly aroma of fungus in the stuffy air. Water from distant springs trickled down in copper-colored rivulets to pool in salty, scummy puddles on the uneven floor.

"If you need refreshment, drink from there," said one of the guards.

"Blaster bolts!" Jacen said in disgust. "You expect us to drink *that*?"

"Not necessarily," said the guard. "But you'll get nothing else from us, so you'd better consider it. If you're hungry, eat fungus. It isn't too poisonous."

One of the mine bosses, a round-eyed Rodian, came up to inspect his new team. He spoke quickly through his tapirlike snout, as if racing to get through a boring memorized speech. "You're here for one purpose: to break stones. You'll never get anywhere close to pure ryll, since the low-grade ore is shipped off planet for chemical separation of the spice. Some of you will use hammers to chip away rock from the walls. It's backbreaking work, and we enjoy watching you suffer."

"What will the rest of us do?" Raynar asked, looking thoroughly intimidated at the prospect of such intense labor.

"That job will be . . . worse," the Rodian said. Reflected light gleamed off his huge metallic eyes. With sucker-tipped fingers, he pointed up to where a network of cables, scaffolding, and fibercords suspended groups of workers under the forest of fungus-covered stalactites. "The rest of you must harvest those rock spikes. Without falling."

As if on cue, two dangling workers broke one of the large inverted pinnacles. The stalactite flew down through the air like a deadly spear to crash into a holding pit far below. Dust and debris billowed up. Guards shouted at the other slaves to keep working.

"We have discovered a new technique," the Rodian said with pride in his thin, warbling voice. "That special fungus you see leaches ryll through the rock and concentrates it in the stalactites. After you break the stone free for us, we can quickly collect the ore in its most valuable form. This helps the Diversity Alliance fund its important activities."

The young Jedi Knights looked at each other, as disturbed at the thought of assisting Nolaa Tarkona's insidious plan as they were to be slaves.

"You—one-armed girl." The Rodian gestured toward Tenel Ka. "Adjustant Advisor Hovrak suggests that I give you the most difficult assignment. To the cables with you . . . and your friend here."

The guards hustled her and Jacen off toward hanging fibercord harnesses, fumbling to fasten the frayed loops around their torsos. A Sullustan supplier handed them each a small vibrating rock hammer.

"What's this," Jacen asked, "a toy?"

"This is your assigned ryll excavating device," the Sullustan said. "It is the most powerful tool you slaves are permitted to wield."

Tenel Ka hefted the puny hammer in her grip, but could think of no way to use it as an effective weapon. None of the surly-looking captives in the mine met the companions' eyes, feigning a lack of interest in the new prisoners.

Using a pulley arrangement, two slaves heaved Tenel Ka and Jacen up toward the jagged ceiling. The floor disappeared beneath her booted feet, and the spiked stalactites rushed down to meet her.

Jaina and Raynar, pushed toward one of the expansive walls, were handed small power digging tools. Glowering armed guards told them to get to work. After a glance up at their companions suspended from the ceiling, the two began to chop halfheartedly at the rockface.

Next to Jaina, Raynar struggled against the unyielding stone. His hands quickly became bruised and bloody from clawing away the loose rock that Jaina broke free. As the son of a merchant lord, he had never worked so hard with his hands. Jaina's hours spent tinkering with mechanical objects had given her just enough calluses to make her tough—but her hands still ached.

"Can't just wait around to be rescued," she said, keeping her voice low. "Nobody knows we're *on* Ryloth. My parents can't send in troops to get us out of here." She heaved a noisy sigh. "That's what we get for not telling anyone where we're going."

Raynar's face was pale, and he looked sick with fear. "Well, Lusa knows. She's our only hope." He swallowed hard. "But she promised not to tell anyone. It may be a long time before she changes her mind."

Jaina gave him a consoling pat on the arm. "We're Jedi, Raynar. We've got the Force. Nothing is ever hopeless. . . ."

* * *

Suspended above the grotto, dangling beside a sharp stalactite, Tenel Ka swung herself into position. She gripped the hard spongy fungus, swung herself like a pendulum, and smashed with her vibrating hammer at the end of each swing.

"I'd love to tell you a joke," Jacen said, swinging himself alongside her so that they stayed close together, "but nothing really seems funny to me at the moment."

They pummeled the same pinnacle of rock until the fungus-covered stalactite broke free and tumbled toward an empty crater in the floor. The rock spike shattered into chunks of rich ore.

"Another one down," Jacen said. "More credits for the Diversity Alliance."

Tenel Ka fumed in silence. Then something caught her eye. With a gesture of her chin, she indicated the chocolate-furred Wookiee woman who had just appeared in an opening in the observation gallery.

Raaba stood tall and enigmatic and powerful. She looked on with interest, turning her attention from one young Jedi Knight to another to another. She spoke with none of the guards, only watched.

Dangling in her harness, Tenel Ka glared in mute fury at this friend of Lowie's who had betrayed them. Then she angrily set back to work, her thoughts as sharp as steel, and as hard.

Finally Raaba turned and stalked away.

Although Tenel Ka hoped to develop a plan, at the moment she had to admit that she could see no way for them to escape.

12

THE SMALL GREEN jungle moon of Yavin 4 was a welcome sight in the *Lighting Rod*'s front viewports. Though thoughts of the Jedi academy still intimidated him, Zekk found his spirits rising in anticipation of seeing his friends Jaina and Jacen Solo again.

He used the entry request code that Jaina had so thoughtfully provided when helping him overhaul the *Lightning Rod* on Mechis III; the New Republic guardian forces in orbit allowed him to pass. Nosing the *Lightning Rod* down into Yavin 4's atmosphere, he wondered if the twins would help persuade Raynar to go along on his search for Bornan Thul. They might even volunteer to accompany him themselves. He hoped that at least Jaina would want to join him.

But as Zekk made his final approach to the Jedi academy's landing clearing in front of the Great Temple, now mostly restored, he felt a strange twinge through the Force. Not a tingle at the back of his neck, as he sometimes felt when danger was present. It was more like a premonition that the day would not turn out quite as Zekk hoped.

Trying to brush aside his sense of unease, Zekk brought the *Lightning Rod* in for a skillful landing on the stubbly grass field. A part of him hoped that the orbiting security force had alerted Jaina of his arrival. If so, Jaina might even now be hurrying down to the landing area to greet him.

To his disappointment, though, he saw not a single familiar face when he stepped out of his ship in the broad clearing. In fact, except for the pair of New Republic guards who patrolled the base of the stone pyramid, no one seemed to take any notice of Zekk's arrival.

Shrugging off his disappointment, Zekk started toward the ancient temple building to find his friends. At the young man's approach, the two New Republic guards—a human and a fish-headed Calamarian—conferred briefly. One pointed behind Zekk at the *Lightning Rod,* while the other consulted a datapad in his hand. Apparently satisfied, the two nodded. The Calamarian offered Zekk a courtesy salute with a broad, webbed hand before the guard's split up and resumed their patrols.

With a pang of guilt, Zekk wondered if Master Skywalker still objected to the military force Chief of State Organa Solo had stationed on the jungle moon, or if he had become resigned to them by now. Zekk himself was partly responsible for the soldiers being assigned to Yavin 4. He had led the Shadow Academy's Dark Jedi in their attack against Skywalker's students.

High above, on the upper levels of the Great Temple, a few engineers and stoneworkers continued the final stages of the pyramid's reconstruction. The upper floors had been blasted away by an Imperial saboteur's bomb. Zekk also felt responsible for the damage the Shadow Academy had inflicted on the ancient Massassi buildings.

Suddenly, as if summoned by Zekk's thoughts, the Jedi Master himself appeared at one of the Great Temple's exterior staircases. With gliding steps, Luke Skywalker came toward him.

Zekk stopped short and struggled to compose himself. He'd expected the Jedi Master to be away on one of his frequent missions. He would have preferred not to face Luke right now. Zekk still had a great deal to atone for.

Master Skywalker had forgiven him for his part in the Shadow Academy now that Zekk had turned away from the dark side of the Force. Even so, it was difficult for Zekk to look the Jedi Master in the face without remembering that he had once been prepared to kill this man and destroy everything he had worked to build. . . .

A warm smile curved the Jedi Master's lips as he clasped Zekk's hand in welcome. But his blue eyes, though kind, held a serious look. "I'm sorry

I wasn't here to greet you," he said. "It's been a busy day of arrivals and departures for us. I only returned from Coruscant a few hours ago, and already I've had to send Tionne and Artoo-Detoo off on a special assignment. After the fall of the Second Imperium, I expected the galaxy to be a quiet place . . . but now it seems *too* quiet; I can sense dark undercurrents, secret plans being drawn against us. I have to be watchful."

Motioning for Zekk to follow him, Luke went back up the broad stairs and into the Great Temple. Once Zekk had stepped into its cool interior, Master Skywalker spoke again. "You have a strong purpose in coming here today, Zekk. Is the *Lightning Rod* in need of repairs again?"

"No, my ship is fine," Zekk said. As they walked along the dim corridors, he tried to tell which parts of the outside walls were original, ancient stone and which had been replaced by skillful craftsmen after the great battle.

Luke Skywalker may have forgiven him, Zekk thought, but did the Jedi trust him? "Actually, I need to speak with Raynar Thul, and Jaina and Jacen."

Luke Skywalker turned to Zekk with a look of surprise. "They didn't send you a message? I only had a couple of hours to speak with Tionne before she left today, but she told me that Tenel Ka received some disturbing news from home several days ago. It must have been something pretty important, because Jacen and Jaina left with her in the *Rock Dragon* to investigate. They took Raynar with them, too."

Zekk was filled with a sense of dismay. "So they're on Hapes, then? Or somewhere on Dathomir, maybe?"

Luke's eyebrows drew together in a frown of concern. "Tionne didn't say. I don't think she spoke with them directly before they left."

Zekk decided to throw caution to the wind. He wasn't sure if Master Skywalker trusted him yet, but if what Zekk suspected was true, then there was no time to agonize over the Jedi Master's opinion of him. He squared his shoulders and plunged ahead.

"I need your help, Master Skywalker," he said. "I've got to find Raynar in the next few days. It may be a matter of life and death—for all of us. It has to do with his father . . . and the Diversity Alliance."

Luke looked probingly into Zekk's emerald-green eyes. Knowing the Jedi could read all of his past guilt and see that the destruction and death he had caused still haunted him, Zekk felt a need to flinch and avert his gaze. But this was too important, so he stood fast and looked steadily back at Master Skywalker.

Finally, the Jedi Master gave a slow nod. "Lusa was the one who told Tionne that the others had left in the *Rock Dragon*. She's an old friend of Jaina's, and recently she and Raynar have become rather close. If anyone knows exactly where they went, it's Lusa."

"Can I speak with her?" Zekk asked. "It's important."

"No one has seen her around the Jedi academy since early this morning," Luke said, "but I'm pretty sure I know where to find her. There's a special place she likes to go."

13

THE QUARTERS THE Diversity Alliance assigned to Lowie were decorated in a style that Raaba had termed "austere opulence." No frills or unnecessary adornments cluttered the area, but the cave chamber and its furnishings were of the highest quality. The rooms were heated to a temperature *almost* comfortable for Wookiees, and the insulfoam that covered the rock walls had been painted to simulate the dark green-and-brown shadows of a thick forest canopy.

The solid Wookiee-sized sleeping pallet bolted halfway up one of the room's walls was as comfortable a bed as Lowie had ever slept in. The unobtrusive lighting could be adjusted to stimulate various conditions, from bright sunlight, to starlight, to pitch black. The sturdy worktable held a state-of-the-art computer station at the perfect height for a full-grown Wookiee. In the corner opposite the sleeping pallet, a massive simulated tree bole swung aside to reveal a fully equipped refresher unit. Nolaa Tarkona had certainly gone out of her way to provide him with pleasant accommodations, Lowie mused.

But for him, these things only served to emphasize that it was all artificial. The underground warren dove deep into the rock of the planet Ryloth. The thin veneer of artificial tree bark merely masked the reality of solid rock beneath solid ground.

The more he learned of the Diversity Alliance, the more these headquarters seemed perfectly appropriate for it. Recruits were shown a thin and civilized veneer of what they most wanted to see—but the true foundation of the Alliance could only be revealed by looking underneath.

Unfortunately, Lowie was not as certain of what lay beneath the Diversity Alliance as he was of the stone in the walls of this room. Lately, it seemed even Raaba was hiding something from him. He could sense that she was holding back when she spoke to him, but she brushed aside all of his probing questions.

Lowie swung himself up onto his sleeping pallet. Then, restless, he swung down again and paced the confines of the room, which seemed smaller to him with each passing day. He could not simply go outside and climb high up to the peaceful safety of the treetop canopy. In fact, there were no trees at all on Ryloth, only agricultural chambers that raised fungus and mosses that were converted into bland but nutritious food.

The closest approximation to forests on this barren planet were the clusters of tall windmills dotting some of the crags. Twi'leks used the turbines to harvest the strong winds and convert them into energy. But most of the wind farms were located on the fringes of the hot or cold zones, in climates so extreme Lowie would have had to wear an environment suit to climb them.

Knowing the room was soundproof, Lowie let out a frustrated roar. If he could not ask Raaba for the answers he needed, who could he ask? Angered, he stopped pacing, turned toward one wall, and pounded a large, hairy fist against it. The cushiony insulfoam absorbed the impact with a soft, unsatisfying *thump*.

Snarling, he snatched the lightsaber from his belt with the vague intention of slicing away the offending insulation. The moment the hilt was in his hand, however, a calm clarity flooded his mind. A flick of his thumb ignited the molten bronze blade.

Lowie gave an *urf* of surprised laughter that, in his anger and frustration, he had been ready to attack a *wall* with his lightsaber! Such was the influence the Diversity Alliance had on him.

He hefted the blade, tossed it experimentally from hand to hand. The saber hummed and sizzled as he sliced the air. Its light shone like a beacon in his mind, illuminating a truth he had known from the beginning: he did not need a

Diversity Alliance to fight his battles for him or to defend his rights.

He drew a bright arc in the air. He did not need "friends" who couldn't accept the friendships he already had. He swung the lightsaber again. He did not need to blame one group for all the misfortunes Wookiees had suffered through the centuries. His species was flexible, strong, capable. They had done well for themselves.

Lowie whirled, sweeping the glowing bronze blade low to the floor. He did not need to hope that others would accept him so that he could find a place where he belonged. He *had* a place. He had friends who accepted him.

Whoosh! Humm! He did not need to find a "cause" to believe in or a direction for his life. He had *all* those things. He was a Jedi Knight!

Lowie's lips peeled back in a feral grin. He felt more like himself now than he had since the day he had met Raaba again on Kuar and found out that she was still alive.

A door signal flashed on the wall. Allowing himself one final sweep of the glowing blade, Lowie switched his lightsaber off, clipped it to his belt, and unsealed the door. It was Sirra, her face alight with enthusiasm. Grasping his arm, she dragged him out into the corridor, telling him that she had something to show him, a magnificent ship.

Giving his sister a quizzical look, Lowie good-naturedly allowed himself to be led along to the small-craft bay. The labyrinth of corridors and tunnels wound steadily upward, and Sirra chattered happily. She had always been a bit jealous that Lowie and his friends had ships they could tinker with together. Now, the Diversity Alliance would make it up to Sirra.

Lowie wondered if Hovrak had finally made good on his offer of procuring a ship for Sirra to fly. If so, perhaps they could soon come and go as they pleased. He was also glad to note that his sister referred to Jaina and the rest of his friends with a sense of fondness, rather than as his "so-called friends" or his "former friends," as Raaba called them.

Sirra explained that Raaba had hinted she shouldn't tell her brother, but there was no way she was going to keep this a secret from Lowie. Besides, Sirra could use his experience if she was going to talk Hovrak into letting her keep the craft. After all, Lowie was familiar with at least one Hapan ship already.

Sirra finally stopped at the entrance to the small-craft docking bay, then keyed in her access code. The hangar-bay door slid open, and with a jolt of shock, Lowie recognized the *Rock Dragon*!

Through a haze of surprise, Lowie heard Sirra ask him if the ship was like the one his friend Tenel Ka owned. She hoped so, since that would make it easier for him to teach her the controls. She was sure Lowie could help her figure it out. But when the dazed look on her brother's face registered with Sirra, she stopped talking. Had she been wrong to show him the ship?

No, he was very interested, he told her. But this ship was not just similar to the one his friend owned—it *was* the ship. The *Rock Dragon,* here on Ryloth.

He asked Sirra if she was certain that Raaba knew this ship was here. Sirra shrugged. Of course; she was absolutely sure. In fact, Raaba had taken her to see the *Rock Dragon* in the first place.

With a feeling of dread, Lowie thanked Sirra for showing him the ship. Struggling to control his anger and uneasiness, he assured her that they would discuss the ship soon. Meanwhile, it was high time he had a heart-to-heart talk with Raaba.

Alone.

Raaba was by herself in her quarters when Lowie burst in without signaling. The young Wookiee woman leaped to her feet when he entered, a guarded look on her face. She ran her fingers through her chocolate-brown fur.

He was surprised when, instead of objecting to his barging in, she asked him if Sirra was with him. He answered bluntly that his sister was still down admiring the *Rock Dragon*—the ship that belonged to his human friends.

Raaba flinched and looked at him defensively, but there was no surprise on her face. This confirmed what Sirra had told Lowie: Raaba had known the *Rock Dragon* was here. She must have recognized the ship when it arrived, and she had not told Lowie about it. Intentionally.

With a menacing growl, he asked if his friends were also on Ryloth.

She flashed him a look of irritation. Of *course* they were here, she snapped. Unfortunately, they had been under some sort of misguided impression that Lowie needed to leave the Diversity Alliance immediately. They had actually managed to sneak into Nolaa Tarkona's headquarters, no doubt with some sabotage in mind, or perhaps intending to kidnap Lowie.

Raaba's voice filled with derision. Nolaa Tarkona herself had pointed out to the foolish young Jedi that she could not allow them to steal Lowie away from his *true* friends. Humans were so arrogant! By breaking into her stronghold, they had proven themselves a threat to security.

Lowie interrupted Raaba. Then why hadn't Nolaa Tarkona simply sent his friends away? Why was their ship still here? Where *were* his friends?

Raaba could not meet Lowie's eyes. She cringed at each question, as if it were a physical blow. Couldn't Lowie see that they were *just humans*? she demanded. They hadn't been hurt in any way, if that was what was bothering him. But surely he understood that Nolaa Tarkona couldn't just let them leave.

Jacen, Jaina, Tenel Ka, and Raynar had broken into the Diversity Alliance headquarters, a deliberately antagonistic act. To let them go

unpunished would be sheer folly. And, mor
important, Nolaa Tarkona couldn't allow anyon
to try to shake the convictions of her loya
followers.

But his friends had come for *him,* Lowie bel
lowed. And he had not *joined* the Diversit
Alliance! Nolaa Tarkona had no right to impriso
anyone who came to see him.

With genuine fear in her eyes, Raaba glance
around in alarm, as if afraid that someone migh
have overheard him. She adjusted her tattere
red headband and urged Lowie to keep his voic
down.

Growling quietly, he demanded in no uncer
tain terms to know where his friends were.

Raaba hunched her shoulders and looked a
the floor. Nothing could help the humans nov
she explained. He had to accept that. She ha
already done everything she could to mitigat
the severity of their sentence. At least they wer
still alive; considering their obvious offenses
mining ryll was the least punishment they migh
have expected. Nolaa Tarkona had said that i
was only fitting—since humans had enslave
so many species over the centuries—that the
should now work to support the Diversity Alli
ance as it struggled to help all oppressed species

Lowie gave a sharp bark of reproof. By sucl
logic, had not humans now become a downtrod
den species under the Diversity Alliance? It wa
obvious that humans were not the only specie
known for their cruelty to others.

Again, Raaba refused to meet his eyes, but she bristled with indignation. Humans had been users and enslavers as long as history could remember; it was only fair that they now reap the crop they had so bountifully planted.

Lowie raised his voice again, not caring anymore who might hear him. Such practices were no more correct now than they had ever been! Jacen, Jaina, Tenel Ka, and Raynar were his friends. Those *humans* in the ryll mines had risked their lives to come here for him! He was going to find a way to set them free—and if Raaba had ever been his friend, she had better not try to stop him.

When Raaba made no answer, Lowie stormed out of the room as abruptly as he had entered.

14

AS HE ANGRILY traced his way through the Diversity Alliance computers, Lowie uncovered false file names, broke passwords, and tracked down all the records he needed to see. With each discovery, he grew more and more outraged over the secrets Nolaa Tarkona had kept from him— and from many of her followers.

His friends had come here to see him, to talk to him . . . but the supposedly compassionate Diversity Alliance had thrown them into the spice mines. As slaves!

All the while, Raaba had continued her sweet words to Lowie, trying to persuade him to join the Diversity Alliance. Apparently, his personal honor and his own wishes didn't figure into her plans. She had hoped to prevent him from talking to the other young Jedi Knights, probably because she was too afraid to let him make up his own mind, to think for himself.

As he scanned a diagram of the complex passages around Diversity Alliance headquarters, Lowie found the vault where his friends' lightsabers had been stored. He memorized the access code. His first step would be to retrieve the precious weapons. Next he would rescue the young Jedi Knights. Then, together, they would all get away from Ryloth.

He'd had doubts before, but no longer. He was completely through with the Diversity Alliance. When Raaba had returned to him, Lowie had been so happy—but now he wished he'd never left Yavin 4.

Computers were Lowie's specialty. He knew how to cover his electronic "tracks." After removing every trace of his searches, Lowie switched off the terminal. He said nothing to the Sullustan computer technicians or the burnished-bronze hacker droids as he left the glassed-in room and set off down the convoluted path to the locked storeroom.

Since he was a respected guest of Nolaa Tarkona, the guards did not challenge him. Lowie had learned long ago that the key to successful bluffing lay in looking confident that you had a right to be where you were and to do what you were doing. He made his way firmly and decisively down winding corridors, taking turbolifts to other levels and passing through restricted areas, until he finally reached the little-used storage vault.

Lowie paused in front of the sealed metal

hatch. A part of him still found it impossible to believe that he had been so completely deceived, and this would confirm—or prove false—all of his suspicions. He flexed his fingers, sniffed the air. His Force sensitivity had been scrambled by his conflicting emotions ever since he'd arrived on Ryloth; it seemed difficult to trust his Jedi training now. But somehow he sensed that he would not be alone here for long, and wasted no time.

His powerful fingers punched in the access code, and the vault door slid aside. Lowbacca's ginger fur bristled as he scanned the narrow metal shelves. He saw three lightsabers inside: Jaina's weapon, fashioned around a power crystal she had grown chemically in her quarters; Jacen's, constructed using a Corusca gem he had mined himself at Lando Calrissian's GemDiver Station; and finally, Tenel Ka's carved rancor-tooth handle. He also saw the utility belt that had been stripped from the warrior girl.

He let a growl build deep in his throat. His friends *were* here—and they were in danger. Scooping up the three lightsabers, Lowie put them in a pouch attached to his syren-fiber belt, then rested his paw on the lightsaber clipped at his waist. This was a time for Jedi Knights to fight together.

Before turning away, Lowie froze as he looked down. He let out a low rumble of surprise. There on the bottom shelf he saw a silvery ovoid, its optical sensors dimmed from loss of power. Em

Teedee had been shut down and stored here as well. The Diversity Alliance, Lowie surmised, was planning to scavenge parts and circuitry from the miniaturized translating droid, or perhaps to search through its memory for weaknesses in humans or in the New Republic.

Lowie crouched low to pick up the translating droid. He looked around warily, anticipating Em Teedee's outburst upon being switched back on. Still sensing no one else nearby, Lowie risked reactivating the droid.

Em Teedee's optical sensors glowed brightly. He burst out in a tinny voice, "Oh, Master Lowbacca! How wonderful to see you again! We've been searching ever so long for you—and oh my, such terrible guards and soldiers! They did horrible things to Mistress Jaina and Master Jacen, and—"

Lowie groaned for the droid to keep quiet and placed a meaty paw over the speaker grille. Em Teedee protested, but Lowie just shook his head and growled a warning about the danger they faced.

Em Teedee fell silent at once, awaiting further instructions.

Lowie's spirits rose. Filled with renewed confidence now that he had the Jedi weapons and his own translating droid, he began on the next part of his plan. Firmly, and with great satisfaction, Lowie clipped Em Teedee back onto his belt, right where the droid belonged.

The stolen uniform of the Diversity Alliance security guard felt stiff and uncomfortable. But Lowie was pleased to note that the black studded sash around his waist, as well as the armored pads on his shoulders, gave him a fearsome appearance. He fluffed up the black streak over his left eye to make himself look even more intimidating—or so he hoped.

He marched purposefully down the corridor and took a turbolift to the excavation levels. Once there, he boarded a high-powered mining car that whisked him off to the mine's nether regions. On the way, Lowie glanced at his chronometer, noting just how many minutes he had before his diversion began.

Plenty of time—provided he didn't encounter any problems.

Em Teedee spoke quickly but quietly; Lowie had already chided him for making too much noise. Still, the little droid seemed determined to express his alarm. "Master Lowbacca, are you quite certain that security uniform you're wearing is necessary? It looks absurd, if I might say so. I simply can't imagine you as the bullying sort. Perhaps we should wait until a better opportunity presents itself."

Lowie grunted, and Em Teedee let out the electronic equivalent of a sigh. "Very well, but if you're so convinced of your importance to Nolaa Tarkona, we've even greater concern for worry. The Diversity Alliance seem to be quite an unsavory lot." Lowie growled his agreement, and the little droid fell silent, as if surprised the Wookiee hadn't argued with him.

The mine car stopped. Lowie did not pause for an instant or show any hesitation. He sprang to his feet and marched briskly toward the noisy, echoing grottoes where, according to the computerized duty roster for slaves, all the new captives had been assigned to work.

Lowie squared his shoulders and strode into the grotto, his alert golden eyes flicking from side to side. Numerous forced labor crews pounded at the rock or shattered stalactites from above. The place smelled of sweat and despair, blood and pain.

The assigned guards were Abyssin, Gamorreans, and other brutish species who seemed to enjoy raining harsh blows upon the prisoners. Bullies developed in all species, and these had found in the Diversity Alliance an opportunity to indulge in the activities that amused them most.

The guards turned at Lowie's brash entrance, grunting guttural questions in various languages, but he bluffed his way forward, knocking them aside. In barks and growls, he demanded to see the shift boss. Finally, the pebbly-skinned Rodian appeared, huge eyes darting furtively around, his sucker-tipped hands tapping with impatience against his legs.

Lowie growled his fabricated orders, but the Rodian hesitated. Em Teedee piped up in an imperious voice, "How dare you delay us, you silly supervisor? Nolaa Tarkona has ordered that the four new captives be brought to her throne chamber. This guard has been sent to escort them."

"But why?" the Rodian said. "Have I done anything wrong? Are they being taken from my charge? I *need* these workers."

"Nolaa Tarkona needs them more," the little droid snapped. "She intends to make a ransom demand. Your immediate compliance is essential for the success of the Diversity Alliance and the glory of our conquest."

The Rodian grumbled and moved to a communications terminal. "I must confirm this with Adjutant Advisor Hovrak," he said.

Lowie roared, and Em Teedee quickly translated, "Indeed not! You are to accept your orders directly from Nolaa Tarkona, without consulting her underlings. To do otherwise will be viewed as insubordination." The droid's voice held an edge of electronic alarm. Lowie simply growled a warning that he would not put much faith in Hovrak's position as Adjutant Advisor anymore, since the wolfman had failed Nolaa Tarkona several times recently.

The Rodian finally backed down and relayed the command in a shrill voice. A few guards snapped to the task, grabbing Jaina and Raynar from a work area near the wall, while two Gamorreans went to pull Jacen and Tenel Ka down out of their scaffolding harnesses up near the stalactite-covered ceiling.

When the four companions were dragged before him, Lowie's heart turned to ice. A cold fury built inside him as he observed their bedraggled condition, their bloodied hands, their dirty skin and haunted eyes.

Jacen looked up as if in fear of another beating, but then recognized his friend. "Lowie!" he cried, but the Wookiee snarled at him to cut off any further outburst and told the miserable prisoner to be silent.

Jaina tossed her long straight hair out of her eyes and looked at him with a stony, unreadable scowl. This meant either that she understood his plan and was playing along—or that she was convinced Lowbacca had been brainwashed by the Diversity Alliance. . . .

He gestured for the four humans to follow him. The Rodian offered additional guards, but Lowie roared and bared his fangs at the mere suggestion that these weaklings could pose any threat to him.

The four weary and aching companions staggered down the corridor, following the Wookiee "guard" out of the mines. Lowie ushered them into a turbolift, closed the door—and then, finally away from prying eyes, gathered them all into a huge bear hug, slapping their backs and howling his joy at the reunion.

He had decided to leave the Diversity Alliance, he told them. He knew what the insidious group was up to now, and he could no longer tolerate being here, no matter how much his friend Raaba wanted him to stay.

"It's not that easy, Lowie. The Diversity Alliance may not let you go," Jacen said. They described Lusa's adventure and how she had discovered that *no one* resigned from the Diversity Alliance. Attempting to leave could mean a death sentence. *That* was what they had come to tell Lowie in the first place.

Lowie just growled. He would find another way out, then, and he vowed to help them all escape from Ryloth. He had a plan to get them out of the tunnels and into the mountains, where he could rescue them.

The turbolift shot upward silently, taking them toward freedom at last.

From the observation gallery above the mine chambers from which he had spied on the captives, Corrsk watched as the Wookiee bluffed the stupid guards and led the prisoners away. Corrsk could have sounded an alarm at any time, because he knew for certain Nolaa Tarkona had given no such orders. Hovrak himself had no idea that Lowbacca had turned traitor and meant to free his human friends. Such news would cause considerable turmoil in the Diversity Alliance, Corrsk knew.

But he had other plans. "Kill humans!" he said under his breath. He let out a long, venomous hiss. "And Wookiees."

He watched, then crept forward. He had anticipated this moment for a long time, but the cold blood of his predator ancestors had taught him patience. He knew how to wait for his prey.

Bloodlust sang in his veins, the scent of Wookiee taunted his nostrils, and nerves tingled beneath his scales. He could be a hero to the Diversity Alliance. He could prevent the escape of the human captives—and if one or two of the prisoners were killed during the recapture . . . surely Nolaa Tarkona would forgive him.

But best of all, Corrsk thought as his vision reddened, he would have his trophy: a fine Wookiee pelt. No one could protect Lowbacca from his claws and his skinning knives now. The Wookiee had turned against the Diversity Alliance, and the Trandoshan would make certain he paid the ultimate price for it.

Corrsk moved quickly out into the tunnels, happy to be on the hunt at last.

15

EXACTLY ON TIME, Lowie's preprogrammed distraction echoed through the tunnels of the Diversity Alliance. Computers triggered alarms everywhere. Sirens blared and lights flashed; a recorded voice requested emergency assistance.

Jacen ducked. "Uh-oh! They know we've escaped!"

But Lowie chuffed with laughter and shook his shaggy head. "Ah, yes. I see!" Em Teedee piped up. "Very clever indeed, Master Lowbacca. I'm sure we're all most impressed."

"What? What's going on?" Jaina asked. Beside her, Tenel Ka crouched, ready to fight with nothing but her bare hand. Yet no attack came.

"Master Lowbacca arranged for the central computer system to activate an emergency alarm that has fooled the sensors into detecting a toxic gas leak in the grottoes farthest from the small-craft landing bay. Emergency crews and security guards will rush in the direction of the alarms whilst—"

Jacen clapped his hands. "While we run the other way! Good thinking, Lowie!"

Tenel Ka nodded. "Excellent strategy, Lowbacca."

Squads of soldiers hustled down side corridors. Fearful alien workers poked their heads out of their chambers. Lowie maintained his alert posture, pretending to guard the four "dangerous humans."

He gave the companions a brief rundown of the main tunnels and airshafts that led directly up to the surface. Some of the passages opened to a narrow band of tolerable temperatures on the surface. The young Jedi Knights would have to make their way up one of the major tunnels to the mountains while Lowie returned for the *Rock Dragon*. Despite the threat of retaliation from the Diversity Alliance, he would find a way to steal the ship, then come pick them up.

"But Master Lowbacca," Em Teedee objected. "Surely this can't be the wisest course of action. Why shouldn't we simply stay together?"

Lowie dismissed this idea as too dangerous. Lowie could pass through Diversity Alliance security; the humans could not.

"Is there no other way to procure a ship, then?" Em Teedee asked. "Why must we risk going back now?"

The Wookiee drew a deep, angry breath and spoke one word that Jacen understood clearly.

"Sirra." Lowie would not leave his sister behind in the clutches of Nolaa Tarkona.

As they ran uphill together, panting, tasting the chalky air with its sour, mildewy stench, Lowie handed his friends back their lightsabers, as well as Tenel Ka's utility belt. Jacen clipped his weapon to his side, as did Jaina, while Tenel Ka kept hers in her hand grip, ready for battle at any moment. She was also glad to have the resources of her belt again. Only Raynar seemed to be at a loss, with no weapon of his own.

Lowie knew exactly where he was going. Tenel Ka studied all the passages as they went, memorizing as best she could the layout of the Twi'lek tunnel systems. Jacen, who ran next to her, was unsurprised to find the warrior girl not the least bit out of breath. Despite the grime that crusted her hair and skin from hours of labor in the mines, he still thought she looked beautiful.

As they rounded a corner, entering the main passageway, they came to an abrupt halt. Three piggish Gamorrean guards marched down the hall, shoulder to shoulder. Their tiny, close-set eyes were devoid of intelligence. The guards grunted and snuffled at each other, upset by the loud alarms ringing in their ears.

In numerous languages, an intercom voice warned of the dangerous toxic gas spill and ordered everyone to evacuate the lower levels immediately. The guards did their best to look intimidating. They pounded on doors and kicked in the ones that remained sealed; some doors opened immediately, and the Gamorreans kicked the occupants instead.

Lowie stood in the corridor, boldly showing off his armor plates and chest band. His streak of dark fur bristled. The four young humans huddled behind him, trying to look like weak and downtrodden prisoners.

Lowie growled a challenge at the Gamorreans. The guards grunted in surprise at this new obstacle. So intent had they been on bashing in doors, they hadn't noticed the Wookiee. The head guard shoved his warty chin and tusks forward. He muttered something in a language that sounded like the burbling of phlegm.

Em Teedee said, "The guard inquires—if I may translate rather loosely—'Aren't you humans?'"

Jacen stepped forward. "Blaster bolts, no! These are only disguises. Part of a top-secret project. Pretty good, aren't they?" Reaching out with the Force, he gave the guards' minds a gentle nudge. "Very realistic." He tugged at one of his cheeks to demonstrate.

The guard snuffled and looked doubtful.

"Yes," Jaina said, stepping up beside her brother. "Nolaa Tarkona's new 'human configuration' disguises. We developed these to infiltrate human cities and governments. But we're really aliens underneath—aren't we?"

Raynar nodded briskly, as did Tenel Ka. "This is a fact," she said.

The guard grunted another question, but Em

Teedee said indignantly, "They most certainly will *not* remove their disguises for mere guards! Indeed! This project is highly classified. I suggest you make yourself useful instead of trying to meddle in affairs that are clearly beyond your comprehension. Go apprehend some fugitive or seal off a toxic gas leak."

The guards grumbled to each other and continued along their way, muttering their admiration for Nolaa Tarkona's cleverness as they took turns banging open doors.

Jacen touched Tenel Ka's wrist to move her hand away from the hilt of her lightsaber. "Sometimes you don't need Jedi fighting skills to take care of a problem."

"Ah," Tenel Ka said. "Aha. But such tricks may not work unless your opponent is as stupid as those guards."

Jacen peered down the surrounding corridors. After a few more minutes of running they reached another main intersection, a confluence of catacombs. Lowie stopped, frowning in distress, and indicated that he had to leave them here.

"Master Lowbacca insists on locating his sister Sirra without delay," Em Teedee said. "I do believe that's quite honorable, though it places us all at greater risk."

Jacen understood that the four humans could not go with Lowie; they had to keep as far away from the alien radicals as they could. Their Wookiee friend regarded each of them fondly. With words and gestures he reviewed for them the directions he remembered from the computer map of the catacombs. They all found it painful to see Lowbacca leave again, but knew that this time he would come back . . . with the *Rock Dragon,* to help them get home.

"We'll meet you outside, Lowie," Jacen called. "In the mountains."

With a last glance over his shoulder, Lowie sprinted down the long winding tunnel into a whirlpool of shadows.

After less than twenty minutes of cautiously toiling their way up the steep passage Lowie had indicated, a complete and deafening silence fell behind them like a curtain. All the alarms shut off; the emergency was canceled.

"That means they've discovered Lowie's trick," Jacen said.

Nolaa Tarkona's voice came over the intercom. "There is no poisonous gas spill. What you just heard was a false alarm, triggered by a traitor in our midst." She paused a moment for effect. "Four human prisoners, important hostages, have just escaped. They must be found. I demand your most diligent efforts in the name of the Diversity Alliance." When Nolaa Tarkona switched off the intercom, her angry voice ended abruptly with the force of an ax chopping through a branch.

"This is trouble," Tenel Ka said.

"We've *been* in trouble," Jaina countered.

Raynar leaned with a heavy sigh against the

corridor's rock wall. "Nobody's going to fall for our 'human disguise' trick a second time."

Tenel Ka suddenly stood up straight. As always, her hearing and eyesight were sharper than any of the others'. She gripped her lightsaber.

An instant later Jacen sensed the approach of numerous enemies. He drew his weapon, as did his sister. The footsteps were coming closer from a single direction, but the tunnels heading away branched out in many other directions.

"Fighting here will be difficult," Tenel Ka said.

Jacen nodded. "We don't have to make a stand here," he pointed out.

"We can run toward the outside," Raynar suggested.

"It'll buy us some time," Jaina agreed. "Let's move."

Clipping their lightsabers to their belts, they raced along the corridors, zigzagging, turning at random intervals as they headed upward. Every tunnel seemed to be filled with thundering footsteps and the rumble of armored feet. The hunt was on in every catacomb; Nolaa Tarkona had no intention of letting the humans escape.

As they picked up speed, the young Jedi Knights dispensed with caution, running as hard as they could. Tunnels branched one direction, then another. Confusing as the choices were, they kept running uphill.

As they plunged across a corridor intersection, they startled a group of five guards—a pair of one-eyed Abyssin, a Duros, and two furry white Talz. All of the aliens bellowed, drew their weapons, and fired.

Blaster bolts ricocheted from the curving tunnel walls, spurting rock dust and smoke. Instinctively, Jaina ducked to one side. Jacen threw himself in the opposite direction as a blast struck the hard ceiling and arrowed back down through the spot where he had stood only a moment before.

"Run!" Tenel Ka said. "Faster!"

They raced along the tunnels, climbing toward the surface as the guards launched after them, still firing . . . still missing. A new alarm sounded; one of the guards must have reported his coordinates and called for reinforcements.

"Do not stop yet," Tenel Ka advised.

"Save the lightsabers for close-in, hand-to-hand fighting," Jaina said.

"I vote we put that off as long as possible," Jacen added.

"I agree," Raynar said, puffing.

More guards joined the chase, converging from different directions. Turning a corner, Tenel Ka spotted a tarpaulin-covered alcove marked with a glowing blue triangle. She recognized the armory symbol immediately. "Aha," she said. "Here." She grabbed the tarpaulin and tore it aside to reveal the small-weapons storage area.

"Are we supposed to just grab some weapons and shoot?" Raynar asked. "I've never fired a blaster before."

The sound of footsteps echoed from several corridors at once. The angry guards bellowed.

"I've got a better idea," Jaina said. She dashed into the alcove and emerged with a thermal detonator in her hand. "We don't have much time," she said. "But I have a feeling this is going to cause a lot of damage. Everybody split up." She gestured in different directions. "Raynar, go that way. Jacen and Tenel Ka, you head down that corridor."

With the time-lock fuse set on the thermal detonator, she tossed it into the weapons storage area, then raced after Raynar. A contingent of guards burst into the intersection and howled as they saw their prey disappearing in two different directions.

But before they could follow, Jaina yelled, "Time!" She pulled Raynar with her into the shelter of a shallow niche in the rock wall. In the opposite tunnel, Jacen and Tenel Ka dove together to the floor.

The thermal detonator went off like a planet exploding.

The weapons storage alcove blasted out with the force of a turbolaser battery. The remaining thermal detonators exploded in a sympathetic eruption. Power packs from the stored blasters added fuel. Rock walls crumbled. Aftershocks trembled through the corridors.

The low ceiling collapsed, and stunned guards tried in vain to cover their heads. Curving walls sloughed into rubble. Smoke and fire gushed in all directions, invading every open pathway.

Feeling the heat singe his jumpsuit, Jacen rolled and tried to cover Tenel Ka's unprotected skin. His ears popped from the overpressure wave.

Within moments the shock front raced past the place where they'd taken shelter. Jacen stood up and brushed himself off. Tenel Ka touched his arm. "Thank you, Jacen," she said. "That was very brave."

"Just my protective instinct," he said with a lopsided grin. He turned to look back up the corridor and discovered that the walls had collapsed, cutting them off entirely from his sister and Raynar.

"Looks like we're on our own," he said.

"We will manage," Tenel Ka answered. "We must get outside, where Lowbacca can find us."

Hearing distant shouts of alarm approaching from an open passage, they limped wearily off down the tunnel before they could be captured again.

Raynar and Jaina plodded ahead. They had not been harmed by the avalanche or the explosion, but they stumbled from exhaustion.

"I hope Jacen's all right. And Tenel Ka," Raynar said.

Jaina could sense that her twin brother and her friend had not been harmed. "They're fine. But we have to put some distance between us and the site of the explosion—all of Nolaa's troops will converge there. Jacen and Tenel Ka can take care of themselves."

"Of course." Raynar forced a smile. "They're Jedi Knights, aren't they?"

"They know where to meet us in the mountains—if we can get out there, that is." They ran uphill, away from the fading dust of the explosion. Neither Jaina nor Raynar had a map of the catacombs, nor did they have Tenel Ka's instinctive sense of direction. But if they continued uphill, they decided, sooner or later they would break out to the surface.

"I think I see light ahead," Raynar said after what seemed like hours. "Natural light."

As if in response, alarmed shouts and nervous blaster fire rang out from behind, though the guards could not possibly have seen them. Yet.

Jaina and Raynar sprinted ahead toward the light.

"It's a passage to the outside!" Raynar said. "We made it."

"But I'm not so sure we want to go there," Jaina replied. "We've gone a couple of kilometers laterally—we may not come out in the narrow temperate zone."

But they hurried along anyway until they reached the opening. A blast of heat struck Jaina's face. She looked out upon the fiery day side of Ryloth, with its unrelenting, pounding sun and scalding-hot rocks. "I've got a bad feeling this isn't where we wanted to be," she said.

Flaming light seared a desolate landscape incapable of supporting life in anything but the deepest shadows. Farther in the distance, cracks and rivers of running lava broke up the landscape. Blackened outcroppings slumped like rotted teeth, eroded by temperatures near the melting point.

Behind them, though, the shouting of Diversity Alliance guards seemed to be coming closer.

Jaina looked out at the hellish landscape, wondering what use the Twi'leks could possibly have had for this opening. Did they send criminals out into the heat to die under the burning sun?

"C'mon, Raynar, we don't have much choice," she said. "Maybe if we keep to the shadows . . ."

Picking their way carefully through the rocky debris, they left the cool tunnels behind and were soon swallowed up by the heat.

Jacen and Tenel Ka stood at the end of the passageway. They had run for kilometers, escaped numerous groups of guards, fled from every approaching noise. Tenel Ka said they had gone through the core of the mountains—and now they stared out a large opening across a glacial landscape with frozen mountains, ice floes, and a night sky so clear and cold the stars looked like chips of ice floating in a black lake.

"We won't survive out there for long," Jacen said with an involuntary shiver. "But we can't survive long in here with those guards and Nolaa Tarkona still after us."

"She will not hesitate to kill us this time," Tenel Ka said. Her lizard-skin armor gleamed in the dim light, but it offered little protection from the cold winds outside.

Jacen stood next to his friend. He and Tenel Ka were both trained in the Force. They weren't completely helpless.

"We have our wits, our lightsabers, our Jedi skills," Jacen said. "We shouldn't need anything else to keep ourselves alive." He smiled bravely. They had to find their way back to the temperate zone somehow and meet up with Lowie.

Tenel Ka nodded. "I agree, Jacen, my friend."

16

LUSA WADED INTO the sparkling green pool at the base of the waterfall. Spreading her arms, she closed her eyes and let the droplets of cool spray caress her face.

There was a strange tingling sensation along the back of her neck. She had always been sensitive to the Force and, though she'd never had much training, she was sure Jaina and Raynar had described this as a sense of impending danger. Raynar, the twins, and Tenel Ka had been gone for nearly six days now. She *knew* something was wrong . . . but what could she do about it?

Lusa waded deeper into the pool, and when the frothing water rose above her flanks, she swam straight toward the pounding waterfall. She had promised Raynar that she would try not to worry for at least three days, and she had resisted the urge to wallow in thoughts of the perils her friends might encounter while rescuing Lowie from the cruel Diversity Alliance. Although each day, the tingling at the back of her neck had returned, each day it had faded again.

But today she could not escape the feeling. It seemed closer than ever.

Letting the pure, cool liquid envelop her, Lusa approached the waterfall. She plunged into it, hoping the cascading stream would wash away the feeling of dread. Water rushed over her and thundered in her ears. Cleansing rivulets sluiced down her bare torso as the heavier flow pounded against her back, easing the tense muscles. The serenity of her surroundings calmed her spirit. Her thoughts were far away on Ryloth, though. . . .

With her back still under the waterfall, she turned to get a better view of the beautiful jungle trees along the shore. To her surprise, she discovered she was not alone, as she had thought. Twenty-five meters away, at the edge of the pond, stood a short New Republic guard she had seen before.

Lusa recognized the Bothan who had accidentally stumbled into the infirmary several days earlier. She wondered if perhaps there was a message in the comm center for her, or if her friends had returned from Ryloth with injuries and the guard had been sent to fetch her.

With a rising sense of alarm, Lusa started to swim for shore. But before she got halfway there, something flew from the hand of the Bothan guard, directly toward her.

A noiseless explosion threw Lusa backward in the water. She tried to flail her arms and found that she could not move them. Furiously, her mind told her four legs to kick—but she could not *feel* her legs.

The sky above her was veiled by a rippling curtain of reddish brown, and she realized that she had sunk beneath the water. Her hair floated before her eyes. She wanted to cry out, but bubbles gushed from her nose and mouth. If she gasped, water would fill her lungs and drown her. She was paralyzed. Her mind cried out for help, again and again.

The next moment, a strong grip pulled her head high above the water and she drew in grateful lungfuls of fresh air. When the hand in her hair gave a vicious jerk, her eyes flew open to find the Bothan's face only centimeters from hers. His expression was filled with hatred.

"Oh, no. You won't die so peacefully," the guard growled. "A traitor to the Diversity Alliance doesn't deserve a peaceful death."

A loud, ominous humming sound sliced past her ear. Lusa rolled her eyes to see that the Bothan held a vibroblade half a meter long in his other hand. She ordered her arms and legs to move, but to no avail. She couldn't speak, couldn't protest, couldn't cry out.

"No, that would be too easy," the Bothan said. "It wouldn't serve Nolaa Tarkona's purposes. You have to *know* that you died for betraying her. And you'll also serve as a lesson to whoever might find your body here."

He slashed the vibroblade through the air in front of her nose, enjoying his position of power. "We can't let a good assassination go to waste and look like an accident. No, this must be reported as a murder. Anyone who hears about it will know that a traitor cannot hide from the Diversity Alliance."

He yanked her head back and touched the tip of the vibroblade to the base of her throat. A few drops of blood welled up where the point pressed into her skin. Lusa tried to shake her head, to strike him with her crystal horns. To her relief, although her arms and legs could not respond, and he still held her fast in his grip, her neck was able to move.

For just a second, a sound distracted the Bothan. The guard's blade wavered and lifted, and he turned to see what had made the noise.

That was all the chance Lusa needed. Ignoring the pain from her pulled hair, she wrenched her head sideways and down and around. With all the force she could muster, she rammed upward, goring the Bothan's furry arm. Blood spurted from the wound. The blood ran into her hair and down her face. She struggled to push her sharp horn deeper.

The traitorous guard bellowed with rage. He lifted the vibroblade high above her, his eyes full of wrath, and Lusa was certain he meant to end her life now, as quickly as possible.

Suddenly, the vibroblade flew from the guard's hand, as if jerked by an invisible rope. Lusa twisted and rammed forward to gore his shoulder this time.

For a moment the Bothan loosed his grasp on her hair. At the same time, the other hand lowered to her throat, but it had dropped the vibroblade. Jerking her head backward, Lusa managed to evade his grasp, but she still could not move her arms or legs. She felt herself begin to sink in the churning water.

The next moment she was raised high in the water by a firm arm beneath her forelegs. The guard dangled two meters above the water in front of her, thrashing furiously with his arms and legs and yelling something incomprehensible in a Bothan dialect.

When Lusa tried to struggle free of the encircling arm, Master Skywalker said close to her ear, "It's all right. I have you. You're with friends now."

At the same moment, the Bothan flew backward and plopped loudly into the shallow water at the edge of the pond. There, a strange young man with long dark hair and flashing emerald eyes slapped a pair of stun-cuffs onto his wrists.

Lusa stopped struggling. Her mouth fell open in surprise.

The young man raised his eyebrows and smiled at her. "Standard bounty hunter equipment. Just a sample of the many things I've learned in my travels." He pulled the bedraggled Bothan upright with a scowl, then looked back at Lusa and Master Skywalker. "This one won't be bothering you again. But when we get back to the Jedi academy, I think the three of us ought to have a private talk—about the Diversity Alliance."

Even using the Force, it took a standard hour for Zekk and Luke to get the injured prisoner and the stunned centaur girl back to the Jedi academy. After they arrived, Luke sent a brief message to his sister Leia about the incident while Zekk dried Lusa off and wrapped her in warm blankets. Master Skywalker entrusted the keeping of the murderous guard to a few New Republic soldiers whom he knew well.

Finally, Zekk, Lusa, and Master Skywalker gathered in Luke's private chambers around a fragrant bowl of steaming soup and a platter of freshly baked bread from the Jedi academy's kitchens. When Luke mentioned that Zekk was a bounty hunter, and Lusa a former member of the Diversity Alliance, the two were instantly wary of one another.

"I'm sorry to have to say this," Zekk said, "but how do we know she's not *still* working for the Diversity Alliance?"

"That Bothan was a Diversity Alliance spy, sent to kill me for leaving. Anyway, how do I know *you're* not a bounty hunter hired to bring me back to Nolaa Tarkona?" Lusa retorted with considerable heat.

Luke intervened. "I think we need to establish some trust here." He looked at Zekk. "I first met Lusa when she and Jacen and Jaina were about five years old. The Force has always been strong in her, and she has been honest with me."

Luke turned to the centaur girl. "And Zekk was once a Jedi Knight. A Dark Jedi, yes—but he came back from the dark side, and the Force is still strong in him. I've looked into both of your minds, and I would trust either of you with my life. Or *Raynar's*." Luke again fixed Zekk with his solemn blue gaze. "Or Tenel Ka's, or Jacen's—or *Jaina's* . . ."

Zekk felt himself flush at the gentle rebuke. Shamefaced, Lusa looked at the floor.

"You're both strong enough in the Force that if you chose to," Luke continued, "you could sense if the other was lying."

Zekk flinched at the reminder. He avoided using the Force, because in the past he had found it so easy to drift to the dark side. But what Master Skywalker said was true: Zekk actually *could* sense that Lusa was an ally, not an enemy. He had to trust her.

"I . . . apologize," Zekk said. "I know how hard it must have been for you to break away from the Diversity Alliance. *I* was once the enemy, too. At one point, I was prepared to fight and kill even the people who had been my best friends—just because I thought I'd found a place where I belonged, a cause to believe in. I found the Second Imperium. You found the Diversity Alliance."

"I didn't realize," Lusa said. "I am sorry. I thought I was the only one who had experienced such things . . . but we each have darkness in our past. I offer no excuse for the things I did: I put my trust in the wrong people and tried to ignore my conscience. I was a fool."

Zekk nodded. "And it's not easy to start a new life once you've been the enemy. I was a fool, too."

Master Skywalker smiled wryly. "Well, now that we've got that settled, we all have information we need to share. First, I'll explain why Tionne left so quickly today. While I was on Coruscant, Leia got a report that a band of musicians sympathetic to Nolaa Tarkona were using their engagements as a cover to smuggle weapons for the Diversity Alliance. Tionne isn't entirely human and, because she's an excellent musician, she volunteered to check out the story. It could be a dangerous assignment, so as an added precaution, I asked her to take the *Shadow Chaser* and Artoo. That's all we know so far."

Zekk spoke next. He stumbled over his words at first, not sure how to explain what he had learned. He told about his initial interest in Bornan Thul as a means to gain fame as a bounty hunter, his assignment to find the scavenger Fonterrat, and what he had learned about Gammalin and the plague. Zekk concluded by describing his encounters with Bornan Thul and his certainty that Raynar's father must be protected from Nolaa Tarkona at all costs.

"Did you hear anything about this plague while you were working for the Diversity Alliance?" Master Skywalker asked Lusa.

The centaur girl shook her head, tossing her glossy cinnamon mane. "I did know Nolaa Tarkona was always searching for power. She made it clear that she would pay well for powerful weapons—or for information on where she could get them. She was even willing to sacrifice a follower or two if it meant getting the resources she needed. At first I thought her noble. Now I know she was merely ruthless."

Zekk suppressed a shudder. "I'm pretty sure that Bornan Thul has the key to where Fonterrat found the plague. But I can't understand why he didn't just turn over the information to the New Republic."

"He probably guessed the Diversity Alliance had infiltrated the New Republic," Lusa said. "The Bothan assassin just proved that to us."

"Shouldn't we put everyone on alert, then?" Zekk said. "We can't trust anybody."

A worried frown creased Master Skywalker's forehead. "That's not as simple as it sounds. It could lead to panic and false accusations. We can't let faithful members of the New Republic come under suspicion just because they're non-humans."

"That may be exactly what Nolaa Tarkona

intends," Lusa said. "If humans in the New Republic start turning on aliens, she can point to it as proof that humans will betray their own allies. It would be the perfect tool to persuade more aliens to join the Diversity Alliance."

"That's why Chief of State Organa Solo and I agreed not to spread the word too widely for now—at least until she's had a chance to question that Bothan guard," Master Skywalker said.

"It's a tricky situation," Zekk agreed. "It could be just as dangerous to distrust the right person as to trust the wrong one. Maybe Bornan Thul wasn't wrong to keep his information to himself."

"Or maybe Raynar's father believed he could destroy the source of the plague himself without telling anyone," Lusa said.

"Whatever his reason," Zekk said, "I came here because I thought Raynar could persuade his father to trust us. Thul is going to need help. I know how to find him now: I have a tracer beacon on his ship. Do you understand why it's so important for Raynar to come back from wherever he went? I need him with me when I go to find his father."

Lusa's eyes filled with tears. "I promised not to tell where they went," she said, "but they were supposed to have been back days ago. They were all willing to risk their lives because they were afraid for Lowie and his sister."

Zekk sucked in a sharp breath. Master Skywalker sat up straight. "Where did they go?"

"Ryloth. To rescue Lowbacca from the Diversity Alliance," Lusa said in a strangled whisper. "They said they'd be back by now."

Zekk's anger at the foolish risk his friends had taken warred with gut-wrenching fear. "Then we'll just have to go rescue them," he said through clenched teeth. He looked challengingly at Master Skywalker, expecting the Jedi to argue with him.

"I don't have the *Shadow Chaser* right now," Luke said matter-of-factly. "We'll have to take the *Lightning Rod*." He looked at Lusa. "You know Diversity Alliance access codes and the geography on Ryloth. Are you willing to help us?"

Lusa shook away the blankets in which she had been wrapped and stamped a hoof on the stone floor. "Yes. I'll come with you."

Zekk started to object, but Lusa flashed him a dangerous look. "Don't even *try* to talk me out of coming along. I want to help our friends just as much as you do." He heard the conviction in her voice, and it suddenly dawned on him that she was no safer on Yavin 4 than she would be in the *Lightning Rod*.

"We're *all* going," Luke said firmly. "We'll need all of our skills, and we'll have to trust each other."

17

THE FIRST THING Jacen noticed before they ventured out into the night side of Ryloth was the searing *cold*. Though the mouth of the cave sheltered them somewhat from the frigid wind, there was no way to avoid it completely. A white cloud of steam formed in front of his face with each breath he released.

The serviceable brown jumpsuit that had kept him barely warm enough while they mined ryll proved a completely ineffective barrier against the deep, gnawing iciness of the eternal winter on Ryloth's dark side.

He shivered and looked at Tenel Ka. Her lizard-hide boots rose to midcalf, but her tough and durable scaled armor covered only a minuscule portion of her upper thigh and left her arms completely bare.

"You must be c-c-cold," he said.

"This is a fact." She reached into her belt

pouch, pulled out the finger-sized flash heater she always carried, and ignited it. Although it was capable of starting a fire—if they'd had anything to burn—the heat it radiated was too small to warm more than the hand that held it.

Jacen wished he had some extra piece of clothing to give her. He toyed briefly with the idea of stripping down and offering Tenel Ka his jumpsuit. But even in the dim light, one glance at the brave face framed by warrior braids told him that he would risk her wrath even to suggest such an idea.

Chill wind gusted into the cave like knives of ice. Unable to think of any other comfort, Jacen put his arms around Tenel Ka and pulled her closer to him, in hopes of at least sharing some of his body warmth.

"It is also a fact that we cannot stay here," Tenel Ka said. Though she was careful to keep the flash heater away from his clothing, her arm slid around Jacen's waist and hugged him tightly. "We must find our way to the temperate zone, over the mountains. I do not believe we have come farther than five or six kilometers from where Lowbacca indicated we should wait for him."

"You m-mean, go back through the tunnels? We'd get lost." He shivered convulsively. "It could take us d-days to find our way back, if we ever do. . . ."

"No," Tenel Ka said. "We would risk being

recaptured." She nodded toward the frigid land-scape outside. "No, we must go out there."

"But you'll f-freeze," Jacen objected. His lips had begun to feel numb.

"I am already cold," she said. "We will grow no warmer by staying in this cave. We cannot hope for rescue if we stay here, and we risk being spotted by the Diversity Alliance."

Jacen's hands, still on Tenel Ka's back, were growing stiff and ached with the cold. He flexed his fingers a few times, then buried them behind the unbraided portion of hair that hung down her back. "You're right," he said. "I just wish we could make a blanket out of your hair."

She jerked backward a few centimeters and looked into his eyes. "Jacen, my friend, that is an excellent idea!"

He blinked back at her, not quite sure how what he had said could actually prove useful. "Please, assist me in unbraiding my hair," she said.

Reluctantly, Jacen released his hold on her; he had enjoyed the close contact. He shook the stiffness from his fingers and tugged a thong from the end of one of her braids. Still clumsy because of the cold, he combed his shaking fingers through her hair to untangle the braid. Handing Jacen the flash heater, Tenel Ka used her single hand with considerably less clumsi-ness. When they were finished, clouds of thick red-gold hair flowed down Tenel Ka's arms, shoul-ders, and back, all the way to her waist.

Tenel Ka looked out through the cave opening, preparing herself for the ordeal they were about to face. Gazing out at the starry sky, she said, "Beautiful. As beautiful as rainbow gems from Gallinore."

"Yes . . . beautiful," Jacen agreed, though he was not looking at the sky.

"We must not delay any longer," she said, stepping outside without hesitation.

"How will we find our way to the temperate zone?" he asked, following her out. The chill sliced into him like a vibroblade. He hadn't thought it was possible for him to feel any colder. But he'd been wrong.

"The day side is that direction," Tenel Ka said, pointing straight through the mountain toward the other side. "Therefore, the temperature zone must be . . ." She pointed up toward the mountain peak that rose above them.

Jacen studied the steep, rocky crag. Its peak, silhouetted by a faint light from behind, must have been four kilometers away—straight uphill. He swallowed, but the freezing wind had stolen all of the moisture from his mouth. Jacen blew on his hands and then folded one underneath each arm to keep them warm. "I can barely move my hands as it is. I'm not going to be able to hang on to rocks. We could probably boost ourselves with the Force, but parts of that slope look too steep to climb, and they're covered with ice."

Tenel Ka looked troubled. "No. Even using my

fibercord will not help us. Our peril would be great. But we *must* find—ah . . . aha!"

Jacen followed her gaze and saw it in the distance: a pass, etched against the sky and mountains in stark relief by a tracing of twilight. The twilight meant that the area must be close to the moderate zone.

"How far do you make it?" Jacen asked. "Seven kilometers?"

She shook her head. "Eight . . . perhaps ten. But our path would be more level. We should not need to climb. I believe we can walk it in a few hours."

Jacen's cheeks and eyes stung from the biting wind. He nodded. "Sure, no problem. You know, I've been saving a special joke for just such an occasion. . . ."

And they set off.

Jacen had lost all sensation in his feet by the end of the first half hour. The rocky ground was often covered with ice. They took turns in the lead, holding a lightsaber high to light the way through the darkness so that they could see the best path to walk. To keep their hands warm enough to grip their lightsabers, they shared the flash heater until its charge ran too low to be of any more use.

At times they had to use Tenel Ka's grappling hook and fibercord to pull themselves over particularly treacherous terrain. Both of them slipped and fell so often that they were badly cut and bruised. After the first hour, Jacen stopped feeling that, as well.

They stayed as close together as possible, blocking the wind for each other from at least one side, and communicated primarily through brief gestures. They kept their mouths closed against the cold and tried not to talk, except when absolutely necessary to decide on a route.

After more than two hours, they stopped where a hillside full of loose rock rose above a slab of sheer, ice-slick stone. They had come a long way already, about two-thirds of the distance, Jacen guessed. But to get to the twilit pass, they would have to cross either loose stones or the slippery rockface.

"We are fortunate," Tenel Ka said, "that we are so close to the temperate zone. Otherwise, we might have been dead by now."

A handful of rocks came loose from the upper slope and skittered down across the steep slab of icy stone.

Jacen gave a halfhearted attempt at a snort. "Yeah, we're lucky, all right." He hadn't been able to tell for nearly an hour whether he still had ears or not. He supposed that it was just as well he couldn't feel them. "Which way?" he asked.

"We could use our lightsabers to cut hand- and footholds into the rock," Tenel Ka suggested.

Jacen nodded. He looked in the direction of the pass toward which they were heading. "What's that?" he said. He pointed to some tall, narrow objects now visible in the pass. They looked like the rigid trunks of scrawny metal trees that had only one or two limbs—limbs that moved.

"Power generators," Tenel Ka said. "The winds are strong in the temperate zone where cold air meets hot. The Twi'leks use wind turbines to run their generators and supply much of their power down in the caves."

Jacen flicked on his lightsaber. "Well, I'm ready to *feel* some of that hot air," he said as a cold wind buffeted them. He swung his lightsaber to notch a few footholds in the icy rock, then stepped forward and swung again.

And so they progressed across the slippery expanse. A powerful gust hit them without warning, knocking them both to their knees on the ice-covered rock. A second gust was followed by a loud clattering noise. Jacen and Tenel Ka looked up in horror as hundreds of small rocks bounced and rolled and ricocheted down the slope toward them.

Jacen switched off his lightsaber. "Look out!" he yelled.

Tenel Ka punched the power stud on her weapon, turning it off. "This way!" she shouted, sitting directly on the ice and throwing her arm around him. Pulling him on top of her, she pushed off down the slope. Like a living sled they slid quickly downhill on Tenel Ka's tough lizard-hide armor, picking up speed and outdistancing the small avalanche.

Fortunately, the smooth rockface did not add significantly to the bruising they had already sustained. Unfortunately, the slope was long and steep, offering no handholds or footholds on the way down. No way to stop.

They slid. And slid . . .

Until they finally tumbled, gasping and panting, onto a broad level area near the base of the mountain. Helping each other up, they scrambled to their feet and ran from the tumbling rocks that followed them down. Within a minute, the tide of rock that had pursued them slowed and stopped.

Panting and shivering, Jacen and Tenel Ka stood for a moment with their arms around each other in the lee of a tall rock. The shelter blocked most of the wind, and—just for a moment—it felt a little less cold.

Jacen was surprised that Tenel Ka did not simply dust herself off and gruffly order him to keep going. Instead, she clung shivering to him for longer than seemed absolutely necessary.

Tenel Ka's loose hair fell forward to cover Jacen's shoulders. He welcomed the extra warmth and snuggled into it. He felt as if he could fall asleep under its blankety softness. He was so cold, so sleepy. . . . He closed his eyes, resting his head on her shoulder. Sleep seemed like a very good idea. . . .

"Jacen, my friend." Tenel Ka's voice was barely above a whisper.

"Hmm?" he asked groggily.

"Jacen, my friend. Tell me a joke."

Jacen's eyes snapped open. Had he really

heard correctly? He put his face close to hers so that he could see her eyes in the starlight. How had he ever thought of her eyes as cool gray? he wondered. Had it taken the contrast with true cold for him to be able to see it? It was obvious now that they were warm, so warm. . . . "Wh-what? What did you say?"

She leaned her forehead against his. "Would you please tell me a joke?"

He smiled, though his lips cracked painfully. "Umm . . . what side of a Wampa ice creature has the most fur?"

"I might welcome the company of even a Wampa ice creature at this moment, and invite it to join our group for warmth. I do not know, Jacen, my friend. Tell me—which side of a Wampa ice creature has more fur?"

Odd, Jacen thought. Tenel Ka must have known this joke. He was certain he had told it to her before. But at the moment that seemed very, very unimportant. Jacen smiled again into the soft red-gold cloud of hair that now drifted across his face. He could feel the Force flowing between them, giving them strength . . . yes, even warming them. "The side with the most fur is the outside," he said.

Tenel Ka shook ever so slightly, though whether it was from cold or from laughter Jacen couldn't tell. She pressed her cheek briefly against his, and whispered, "Thank you, Jacen, my friend." Then, releasing him, she took one of his hands in hers.

Jacen looked around the rock toward the pass that led to the temperate zone. "We lost ground," he observed.

"Yes, but only a little. The pass should not be more than an hour's walk now. Our path appears clearer and easier—with a short climb uphill at the end," Tenel Ka pointed out. "We can make it, Jacen. We must continue."

Jacen believed her. He felt a new spring in his step as they left the shelter of the rock. They passed many caves or tunnel entrances—Jacen couldn't be sure which—but the ground was solid. On the slopes ahead they saw the strange mechanical towers of wind turbines erected by the Twi'leks. The structures appeared ancient, but still functioned. Jacen wondered how often any of the tunnel inhabitants braved the cold temperatures to service the turbine mechanisms.

The wintry air took its toll as they continued. Jacen's mind began to go numb. He had entered a trancelike state and had no idea how he kept putting one foot in front of the other. He was in the lead, holding his lightsaber aloft, when Tenel Ka put her hand on his arm and pulled him to a stop.

"What is it?" he asked.

She nodded toward the frozen peaks above them; gaps in the crags showed the line of twilight in the distance. But the air appeared to ripple as if alive. Shimmers of light contorted and danced through the air in an invisible undulation that seemed to make the icy rock surfaces ripple like an ocean.

Suddenly, a jet of steam half a kilometer high spewed upward from the frozen ground where the shimmering waves touched down. It seemed like a whirlwind, a spinning mass of displaced air and wind roaring over the mountains and sweeping toward them.

"Heat storm," Tenel Ka said tersely. "I have read about them."

"Heat?" Jacen asked, feeling hopeful.

"Heat *storm*," Tenel Ka warned. Her grip tightened on his arm. "Hot winds from the daytime side of the planet. They can travel through the temperate zone to the night side and still retain enough heat to boil alive any creature in their path. We must find shelter."

The shimmering waves swirled, forming a superheated funnel cloud that began whirling directly toward the side of the mountain. Rocks shattered, ice evaporated, and scalding, shrieking wind plowed through side canyons with a battering ram of displaced temperature.

"The caves!" Jacen yelled, grabbing her hand and turning back toward the last tunnel entrance they had passed, beneath one of the old wind turbines. Together they ran, forgetting caution on the rough ground.

The hot whirlwind climbed the slope toward them, howling like a vengeful spirit.

When he saw the broken entrance a few meters ahead of them, Jacen switched off his lightsaber and concentrated all of his efforts on speed. Not a minute too soon, he and Tenel Ka threw themselves into the narrow mouth of the cave. The furnace-hot blast roared toward them, flash-evaporating ice. Rock cracked and crumbled.

Jacen and Tenel Ka backed up to where the dark cave widened out and pressed themselves against the rough stone wall. Hot wind buffeted the rock outside, melting ice and sending up sizzles of steam, but the narrow-mouthed cave protected them somewhat.

Sinking wearily to the floor, Jacen said, "I didn't know I had the energy left to run." The storm grew louder, closer, as if angry that they had escaped.

Beside him, Tenel Ka looked around suspiciously. "Jacen, my friend—we are not alone."

18

FEIGNING A CALM nonchalance, Lowbacca led his sister Sirra through the tunnels toward the small-craft bay where the *Rock Dragon* waited. The Diversity Alliance engineers had not managed to crack its access codes yet. They could not get into the ship's main memory, activate the hyperdrive controls, or set a course in the navicomputer. But Lowie knew the codes. He and Sirra could use the *Rock Dragon* as an escape vehicle. They had few choices at this point. He had to get his friends away from Ryloth and Nolaa Tarkona.

Lowie hoped the preprogrammed warning sirens would keep the Diversity Alliance soldiers occupied. Technicians, dock workers, inventory control officers, and maintenance engineers ran through the tunnels, panicked by the alarm klaxons.

Lowbacca had stripped off his guard armor

and tossed it down a waste chute into an underground well. He smoothed his black streak back with a brush of his hand, and once again looked like a studious Wookiee who spent too much time around computers.

Lowie had found Sirra diligently helping out in a loading bay. She hadn't seemed to mind the hard work of lifting pallets of materials in sealed containers labeled FOOD or MEDICAL SUPPLIES to be taken to downtrodden alien worlds. And she had been glad to see him.

Lowie had pulled her aside and breathlessly told his story of betrayal. The truth had been kept from them, he explained; the young Jedi Knights were being held captive down in the spice mines. Sirra was shocked at the news, and reluctant to believe it. But she had seen the *Rock Dragon* herself, Lowie reminded her. Em Teedee's very presence substantiated his story. How else could Lowie have gotten his translator back, since he had left the little droid on Yavin 4?

Lowie crept behind one of the supply crates and motioned for his sister to follow him. The other workers, intent on the blaring alarms, took no notice of them. Lowie punched his fist through the side of a crate, breaking a hole in its thin veneer to reveal not medicinal supplies or food, as the labels declared, but power packs for long-range, military-style blaster rifles.

Sirra swallowed hard; her shaved patches and tufts of fur stood out prominently in all directions. She picked up one of the blaster packs and stared coldly at it.

"I believe Mistress Sirra will require no further demonstration of the veracity of your claims," Em Teedee said.

Sirra groaned, realizing that Raaba herself must have known the truth. Lowie growled in sympathy. He wanted very much for Raaba to see the light, to escape with him and Sirra—but their Wookiee friend was too much a part of the Diversity Alliance and its plans.

As Lowie and his sister left the loading dock behind and made their way toward the small-craft bay and the *Rock Dragon,* he found himself wondering if the young Jedi Knights had found their way to safety in the mountains by now.

When the false sirens fell silent, though, Lowie realized instantly that they were in trouble. He grabbed Sirra's patchwork-furred arm and dragged her forward. They raced down one level, then through a long corridor. Just as the doorway to the vehicle bay loomed up ahead of them, tantalizingly close, Nolaa Tarkona's angry voice burst over the intercom, declaring the presence of a traitor in their midst.

Em Teedee wailed, "We're doomed! Oh, my! Whatever shall we do?"

Lowie growled a response that did not require any translation. His heart sank. He had left his human friends to fend for themselves, and now they would be pursued harder than ever. At least his false emergency had given them a small head

start toward the surface. That was all the time
he'd been able to buy them; he hoped it was
enough.

The minimal Diversity Alliance crew still working in the small-craft bay came to attention as
the two Wookiees approached. Lowie took a deep
breath. Before they could enter, though, a hulking form stepped out of the shadows and blocked
their way. The giant reptilian form of Corrsk
filled the passageway. The Trandoshan held a
blaster cannon powerful enough to fry both Lowie
and Sirra to ragged, smoking hunks.

"Traitors die," he said in a rough, gargling
voice. "Kill Wookiees!" His fang-filled jaws flexed
in a vicious grin. He brought his blaster cannon
to bear. "These are traitors!" Corrsk bellowed,
glancing over his shoulder to the workers in the
small-craft bay.

Two Duros star pilots and a group of Ugnaught
mechanics turned to stare at the commotion.
One ran to a comm panel and called for security
backup.

Corrsk did not appear interested in sharing
the glory for the prizes he had captured.

Lowie drew his lightsaber and ordered Sirra to
make a run for the *Rock Dragon* as soon as she
saw a chance. Without the access codes she
wouldn't be able to set any course, but she could
prepare it for flight. He shoved his sister behind
him as he switched on his molten-bronze blade.
Then, holding it aloft like a powerful, glowing
club, Lowie advanced toward the enormous rep-

tile, taking the offensive against his natural enemy.

Corrsk drew back in surprise and lifted his blaster cannon, firing a shot before he had a chance to aim. Lowie dodged out of the way as the ragged bolt of energy hammered the tunnel wall.

Sirra used the moment of distraction to sprint past Corrsk into the small-craft bay and make a beeline for the Hapan passenger cruiser. Two Ugnaughts tried to block her way, but she bowled them over, batting one to the side with her left paw and knocking the other down with the sheer force of her charge.

The *Rock Dragon* waited, a sanctuary, their escape. Sirra had admired the ship, had hoped someday to fly it. She would soon get her chance.

Lowie charged at Corrsk with a furious roar. He swung his lightsaber. The Trandoshan, more agile than his size suggested, skipped to one side. Lowie's sizzling bronze blade sheared through a metal support beam on the wall and gouged a smoking crater into the rock.

He reeled backward, raising the lightsaber again as Corrsk struggled to aim his blaster cannon. Lowie felt a tug and a snap at his syren-fiber belt, and Em Teedee pulled free, rising up on his new microrepulsorjets.

Lowie yelped in surprise. "I beg your pardon, Master Lowbacca," the little translating droid said, "but I must have neglected to mention some of my more recent modifications."

Em Teedee zipped forward and back, dancing like a target remote in front of the reptilian. Corrsk batted at the little droid with a scaly hand. One curved claw clipped the silvery casing and sent Em Teedee tumbling and spinning.

"Oh my, how very disorienting!"

Lowie slashed with his lightsaber while Corrsk's attention was still on Em Teedee. The Trandoshan tried to dodge, but the edge of the molten blade scorched his scaled arm. Sizzling black blood congealed in the wound. Corrsk hissed with pain. He lifted his blaster cannon and launched a high-powered volley.

Lowie reacted with Jedi reflexes, bringing up the bronze blade to meet the blaster strike. The force of the blast drove him against the wall, but the energy blade deflected the barrage back into the rock ceiling above Corrsk's head.

The reptilian let out a bellow as tons of rocky debris cracked and broke away from above. He threw his massive arms overhead, trying to protect himself from the falling boulders. Giant chunks of rock tumbled down in a deadly avalanche to bury him.

With Corrsk foiled for the moment, Lowie did not hesitate: he turned to charge after his sister into the small-craft bay. Sirra, already aboard the *Rock Dragon,* was prepping it for takeoff. He heard the familiar whine of engines; a white flare of exhaust heated the grotto.

Heavily armed guards, summoned by the Ugnaughts, rushed in with hand weapons. They saw Lowie and fired. He dodged across the cluttered room, ducking and weaving around engine parts and coolant drums, using his Jedi senses to anticipate their shots.

Em Teedee zoomed after him across the grotto in a zigzag pattern. "Do hurry, Master Lowbacca! I'm right behind you!" Lowie made a mad dash toward the Hapan cruiser. Several of the guards' potshots struck the hull of the *Rock Dragon,* but the hand weapons did not have enough power to cause significant damage.

Lowie scrambled up through the entryway and into the cockpit. As he slid down into his familiar copilot's seat, he wished briefly that Jaina were there with him. Fortunately, he had no doubts about Sirra's ability as a pilot. She almost seemed to be enjoying the challenge of their dangerous situation. When she flashed her fangs at him, Lowie remembered watching her practice her wild flying skills in the skies above Kashyyyk. He had every confidence in his sister's abilities. At the moment, though, he had grave questions as to how he would rescue his human friends, and whether he could ever free Raaba from this tangled web into which she had fallen. . . .

With an electronic sigh of relief, Em Teedee zipped into the cockpit and dropped down onto the control panels. "Assistant navigator, reporting for duty! Might I recommend an immediate departure?" he said.

Roaring his agreement, Lowie sealed the *Rock Dragon*'s entry hatch while Sirra punched up the

engine controls. The repulsorlifts barely had
time to raise the craft off the ground before Sirra
launched the ship forward. One of the landing
struts scraped a white gash along the stone.
Lowie dragged himself into the cockpit and frantically began entering access codes and connect-
ing Em Teedee's wiring to the navicomputer.

The *Rock Dragon* shot toward the blast doors,
which were even now closing as a few Ugnaughts
furiously cranked mechanical systems to seal the
Wookiees in. But Sirra put on a burst of speed
that threw Lowie back in his seat.

From the outer tunnel, where the Trandoshan
was now completely buried, more guards raced
into the bay to set up heavier weapons on tri-
pods. They fired before they were ready, though,
and only struck the blast doors and walls. The
Duros, Sullustans, and Ugnaughts dove for cover
from the ricochets.

Sirra let out a howl of triumph as the ship
skimmed through the narrowing gap of the closing blast doors. The *Rock Dragon* soared out into
Ryloth's open sky.

In the dust-filled tunnel, salvage workers scurried across the rubble, picking at the rocks and
hauling away fallen boulders in order to open the
collapsed passageway.

With a clatter of broken stone and a mighty
roar of anger, the Trandoshan burst through the
avalanche debris and hauled himself out of the
rubble. He coughed and spat. Blood leaked from

gashes in his tough, scaly hide. Filth encrusted the burned wound where Lowie's lightsaber had scorched him. Corrsk didn't feel any of it.

Two furry Bothans tried to help the reptilian, but he hammered them aside and climbed to his feet.

His left leg was terribly injured. Corrsk looked down at his mangled scales and crushed muscles with anger. Still, he felt no pain. He let out a snarl as he saw that the *Rock Dragon* had escaped through the closing blast doors. The ineffective guards shot their clumsy weapons again, but to no avail.

Corrsk clenched his clawed hands. He desperately needed to kill something, *someone,* and he wanted it to be one of the Wookiees.

The smell of Lowbacca's blood was in his nostrils now. The Wookiees had injured him. Corrsk would not stop until he was able to crush Lowbacca with his bare hands.

19

PUNISHING HOT LIGHT poured like a river of fire down from the sky, and Ryloth's surface radiated it upward again in shimmering waves. The sweltering day-heat was intense, rolling off the dark rocks and the half-melted sands. Every breath was like gulping a mouthful of fire. Ryloth's unmoving sun burned a bright hole in the sky and reflected from every object on the surface. Far from the sheer cliffs, chasms split open like old scabs to reveal running streams of molten lava that burned orange, yellow, and white.

Raynar did his best to keep up with Jaina as they trudged between cracks, leapt across open spaces like ovens, and hid from the fire in any shadows they could find. "Now I know—what a nerf sausage—on a hot plate—feels like," he panted.

Jaina couldn't answer. Her skin was already red and raw, her hands and feet blistered. The temperate zone seemed impossibly far away across the broiling landscape. Jaina didn't know how they would ever get there, or if Lowie had even made it safely to the *Rock Dragon*.

With sunken cheeks, red-rimmed eyes, and dry, salt-encrusted skin, Raynar looked completely desiccated. His hair and his jumpsuit would have been drenched with sweat, had the searing heat not evaporated all perspiration the moment it appeared.

"Remember how comfortable the tunnels were?" Raynar said as they worked their way along the mountainside, trying to climb higher to safety, to the temperate zone. "The shade, the walls that were cool to the touch . . . the shadows, the air you could breathe . . ."

Jaina trudged ahead. "Sure. And Diversity Alliance soldiers hungry for our blood . . ."

"Well, that was *one* drawback," Raynar admitted.

Jaina climbed up a rockface, along a cleft in the stones that provided some shade. She slipped briefly and, reaching out to steady herself, touched an outcropping exposed to the direct sunlight. Jaina hissed in pain and snatched her fingers away. Red burn-welts sprouted on her skin.

"Working the mines is starting to sound like a vacation to me," she admitted. "We don't have any water out here, no food or protection. . . ."

Raynar spoke in a whisper so he wouldn't have to inhale much of the hot air. "Maybe Lowie can still find us. You think he made it out in the *Rock*

Dragon? You think Jacen is safe? And Tenel Ka?"

Jaina continued climbing upward, grimly seeking a cave or cleft that would offer them temporary shelter from the unending day's fire. "We've had other plans that were a bit more successful," she said.

"I need to rest . . . just cool off for a little while," Raynar said.

Spying a crevice, Jaina ignited her lightsaber and hacked away at it, chopping out huge glassy lumps of stone. Raynar pulled the rocks aside to deepen the small alcove, to deepen the shadows.

Jaina's lips were chapped and dry. Her tongue felt thick and her throat was like sandpaper. She was desperate for a drink, any kind of drink.

Dazzled by the brilliant sunlight, she fixed her eyes on the rock, daring to hope that she might accidentally break through to a natural spring in the mountainside.

The lightsaber sizzled as Jaina worked, shedding its eerie violet light into the alcove. Raynar helped until Jaina finally gave up, panting and shuddering with exhaustion. "Rest here—in shade—for a while," she gasped. Together, they crawled into their tiny shelter.

Raynar sighed. "It'll never get dark on this side of the planet. It always stays hot. Are you sure we can't just go back and surrender?"

"Absolutely not." Jaina fixed him with the most valiant stare she could muster. "We're Jedi Knights, Raynar. We'll think of something." She hunkered down against the rock wall of the new alcove. Even here in the shade, deeper in the rock, fingers of the throbbing heat reached toward them . . . but at least it was a few degrees cooler. "We'll wait here until we can figure out what to do."

Raynar sat next to her in silence.

Where the Diversity Alliance tunnels opened to the glaring sun of Ryloth, Hovrak stopped and paced. Many Twi'lek prisoners and defeated clan leaders had gone out this doorway, exiled to die in the Bright Lands.

But no one ever went out there *voluntarily*.

He had followed the stench of humans all the way here from where he had picked it up in the lower tunnels.

One of his lieutenants spoke. "Are you certain the humans came here, Adjutant Advisor?"

"Of course," Hovrak growled. "Can't you smell them?"

The scent of prey filled his nostrils, though blood still clogged his nose from where Tenel Ka had punched him the day before. Even injured, the wolfman could easily detect the stink of humans. They had fled out into the heat. They were fools to think they could survive in that environment.

One of the Talz guards spoke up next, his voice squeaking through the tiny mouth at the end of his proboscis. "They must have burned to death by now."

Hovrak bared his fangs and shook his furred

head. "Others have made such erroneous assumptions, but I will not be one of them. I won't be satisfied until I see their charred and dehydrated corpses frying in the sun."

The Adjutant Advisor gave an order and turned to stare out into the oppressive sunlight as his assistants scurried to follow his instructions. Before long, several Diversity Alliance workers rushed to the end of the tunnel, carrying bulky, heat-reflective suits. The silver polymer material was shiny, like a mirror, to deflect the blazing sunlight.

Hovrak grabbed a suit and studied its configuration to make sure it would fit his body type. Taking care not to knock loose any of his precious medals, he tugged the suit on over his formal uniform and directed four of his guards to do the same.

Hovrak sealed his transparisteel helmet and stared through its mirrorized coating. Now he could walk and see comfortably, even out in the harshest glare. The suit's recirculating climate-control systems kept him cool, and he listened to the hiss of cool air as he breathed. The four guards, now suited up, gathered beside him, anxious to begin stalking. They wanted to kill the escaped humans before the searing heat did the job for them.

The landscape out there was hellish: fire and lava, rock and desert. The silvery suits would protect them against far greater extremes than the weakling humans would be able to endure.

"Let's go," Hovrak said through the comm unit in his helmet. "No one rests until our task is finished." The Adjutant Advisor stepped out into the sizzling daylight, looking for any shadowed path that Jaina and Raynar might have chosen to walk. The two humans could not have moved very fast across the treacherous landscape, picking their way upward; they could not have gone far.

Hovrak shouldered his weapon, hoping that its circuits wouldn't be scrambled by the unaccustomed inhospitable temperatures. Of course, if the blaster refused to fire, he could simply attack the young humans with his hands. The rocks felt soft and plastic under his heavy-booted feet. He grasped outcroppings with his gloves to help himself along, and easily picked up the trail. The humans hadn't had many options.

A couple of the Diversity Alliance guards appeared uneasy, less confident than he was in the protective abilities of their suits. Hovrak ignored their concerns, though, and snarled through the helmet comm system for them to hurry up.

When he caught the humans, Hovrak would have to restrain himself from killing them too quickly. The heat, the sunlight, the lava offered numerous possibilities for drawing out their pain. Nolaa Tarkona would be so pleased.

Armored against the heat, the silver-suited hunters moved steadily along, closing in on their prey.

20

AS THE HEAT storm howled past the frozen cave opening, Jacen listened to the cracking, scalding wind. Suddenly superheated rock tumbled free outside and ice formations melted.

Clouds of mist roiled at the entrance like soup, making the air dense and impenetrable in Ryloth's frozen night. A jet of steam shot into the cave, struck the wall, and froze instantly into a hard, glassy coating. Gusts of raw, hot air struck Jacen in the face, but his skin was so numb he could take no pleasure in it.

Behind him, Tenel Ka was more intent on the sound she had heard from deeper within the cave. "Who is there?" she said. "I sense you here with us." She drew her lightsaber and switched on the humming beam as the storm continued to rage outside. Her turquoise blade cast a dim blue-green glow.

"So, someone has come to kill me at last," a

hoarse voice rasped. "I would have managed the job myself eventually . . . if you had given me a little more time."

As the wind whipped the mountainside, Jacen heard a mechanical rattling from the windmills and turbines that stood sentry like robotic scarecrows outside. The inescapable force of the whirlwind spun gears and powered the generators. Jury-rigged lights inside the cave flickered on to reveal an extensive network of living chambers.

Jacen stood next to Tenel Ka, ready to fight. He drew his own lightsaber, planning to ignite the emerald blade, but he quickly saw they had nothing to fear.

Back in a cleared section of the cave huddled an old Twi'lek man. His face was gaunt, his skin bruised and grayish. He looked up at them, head-tails trembling as if from the cold. He blinked repeatedly. His once sharpened teeth were now dull and cracked.

The Twi'lek drew himself taller, gathering together his few ragged scraps of pride. "This is all that remains of me and my once great clan," he wheezed. "I should have followed the others into the Bright Lands, but Nolaa Tarkona cruelly exiled me to the cold. I could not make the long journey across the shadows and into the purifying sun."

"Who are you?" Jacen asked. "What's your name?" Overhead, the wind turbines spun and vibrated, powering the haphazardly propped glowpanels.

The Twi'lek took a deep breath. "I am Kur . . . ," he said, then hesitated. "Just *Kur*. I have no clan name any longer. It has been stripped from me."

"Nolaa Tarkona did that to you?" Jacen asked.

The Twi'lek turned his face away, as if unable to bear the truth.

Tenel Ka switched off her lightsaber and answered for him. "When a clan is defeated, the five clan leaders are exiled to the daylight side of Ryloth. In the Bright Lands, at the mercy of the heat, they soon succumb to death."

"But Nolaa threw me to the cold wastes instead," Kur said. "I have eked out a living, under these generator stations that provide power and air circulation for the caves below. But most of the large Twi'lek cities are far from here. Nolaa Tarkona selected an isolated area for her headquarters. From there, she keeps the rest of my people living in fear."

Seeing no actual danger from Kur, Jacen and Tenel Ka crept deeper into the cave, seeking shelter from the crackling cold outside. To Jacen, the warrior girl's skin appeared translucent and blue from the frigid temperatures . . . not to mention banged, bruised, and scraped from their rough fall across the rocky ice field.

He wasn't much better off himself, but at least he'd had his comfortable coverall to give him some protection—much more than Tenel Ka's reptile-skin body armor had offered.

The Twi'lek exile stood up. He reached back

around some rocks near a flickering glowpanel and pulled out a tattered, worn strip of hide, a very meager blanket. "Here, girl, use this. It's the best I can offer."

Tenel Ka took the blanket, which Jacen helped her drape over her shoulders. She hunched down to conserve her body heat, and Jacen huddled next to her, adding his warmth to hers.

"When I came here to this place, I found one weak and starving rylcrit," Kur said. "Deep in the caverns of some of the larger Twi'lek cities, my people raise those hardy animals for meat. But this one had survived out here in the wastelands. It died soon after I found this cave. I ate the rylcrit meat over the course of a month. I used its bones to make tools and its hide to make the blanket. May it warm you enough to survive for another day."

Tenel Ka's voice was gruff, almost defiant, despite the shivering she tried to control. "We *must* survive another day," she said. "We must escape."

Kur chuckled, a sound like crumbling dry leaves. At this, Jacen stiffened and took offense. "We *will* get out of here," he said. "We've got a ship coming."

"So you expect to get off of Ryloth?" Kur said. "Then someone must have given you false hope."

Jacen glared at the Twi'lek. "How did Nolaa manage to take over all your cities?" he asked, changing the subject. "She doesn't seem to have many Twi'lek followers in her Diversity Alliance.

In fact, considering the large populations in some of the cave cities, I'm surprised she has any control over them at all."

"Nolaa Tarkona is an anomaly in many ways. Twi'lek culture has ancient traditions. Our power is distributed among the clans and cities. We maintain that power through cleverness, deceit, wily tricks . . . rather than through violence and force.

"But Nolaa Tarkona doesn't play by our rules. She escaped from slavery, gathered her allies, and came to our tunnels with a small army. She attacked without warning and overthrew the clan leaders. Some she sent down into the ryll mines, others she killed outright. For me she reserved a special punishment. I was exiled here instead of being sent to the Bright Lands, where I should have gone to become part of the fire."

Kur looked down at his clawed hands. His head-tails trembled as if he were experiencing some sort of seizure. "I always intended to make the journey, but I never quite . . . managed."

"Then you can help us make it to the temperate zone?" Jacen asked. "We need to get out of here and up to where our friend can find us. We have lightsabers to signal with. We know he's coming."

"It is a long way," Kur said. "And very cold."

"It is cold here in this cave," Tenel Ka pointed out. "If I must be cold, I would rather be moving toward a goal."

Kur looked around his squalid chambers. His home in exile. The heat storm had passed now, and the creaking, spinning wind turbines began to slow. The lights in the chamber dimmed.

With a sigh, he pried up some loose chunks of rock, under which grew a spongy, feathery patch of lichen, veined with blue and red. "You must eat this," he said, tearing off a scrap for himself. "It is the only food I have, and we will need all our strength to attempt this insane journey."

Jacen took the tart, tough lichen and chewed on it. After the brackish water and the bitter fungus they had had in the spice mines, he had no complaints about anything that was meant to give him sustenance.

Tenel Ka ate her share without comment.

"If we are to make progress," Kur said, "we should set out immediately, in the wake of the heat storm." He stood, and his arms trembled weakly. "We will probably freeze to death out there . . . but for a short while we will have a small amount of residual warmth to help us along."

Jacen steeled himself for their venture back out into the bitter cold and wind. He cleared his throat.

"Well," he said bravely, "what are we waiting for?"

The landscape had changed dramatically in the aftermath of the capricious storm. The hot whirlwind from the day side of the planet had blasted across ice patches and glacier fields, leaving spearlike icicles flash-frozen to the rugged cliffsides. Evaporated water that had crystallized in the air now blew around them as dry, scouring snow.

Kur kept his head low; his head-tails twitched around his shoulders as he trudged along the stony slopes toward the faint glow several rugged kilometers in the distance.

The snow that swirled around them blinded Jacen. He took Tenel Ka's arm so that they wouldn't get separated. Once, when they became disoriented, he ignited his lightsaber and let the emerald green blaze like a torch. Snow sizzled as it struck the energy blade. The wind whistled and howled around irregularities in the cliff faces.

As they climbed higher, the breezes grew more severe, and the biting cold drained Jacen's energy. Every step seemed nearly impossible. Slogging through a sea of weariness, he pushed himself to go farther and farther. In his mind, he cried out with the Force, "Lowie, we're here . . . don't give up looking for us!"

Tenel Ka stumbled, and Jacen helped her up, only to find that she had tripped over Kur, who huddled on the ground in despair, refusing to go on. Together they pulled the old Twi'lek to his feet. "Can't rest now," Jacen said. "You won't make it to the Bright Lands."

Kur moaned. "Then I'll just die here."

"That is not an option," Tenel Ka said.

The night sky cleared again, showing a spray of stars. All the snow created by the heat storm blew away, gathering in small mounds against the cliffs. Jacen was dismayed to see that their destination appeared no closer than it had seemed hours before.

Tenel Ka pulled in a deep breath. "Master Skywalker once described techniques a Jedi can use to endure cold or heat," she said. "We must use these skills now."

Jacen nodded jerkily. "Our friend here doesn't have those abilities, though."

"Then we must help him reach the temperate zone before it is too late."

The slope grew steeper, rockier, but still they kept moving toward the line of distant twilight. Tenel Ka once again had to use her fibercord to help them to climb between rocky pinnacles. With his lightsaber, Jacen cut sturdy footholds into the caked ice inside shallow crevices.

The two companions pushed and dragged the old Twi'lek exile, urging him to climb higher. "Just a little farther, Kur," Jacen chanted in a voice that was barely more than a whisper. "Just a little farther."

But when they finally reached the top of the ridge, Jacen's heart dropped. A sheer gorge and a landscape of cracked hills blocked their path to where the twilight lands would offer them safety.

"We'll never make it across that," Jacen said in dismay.

"This is a fact," Tenel Ka agreed. Her voice was flat, but Jacen heard her despair.

Where would they find the strength to go farther? They were exhausted, freezing. The Twi'lek had slumped into an unconscious stupor beside them. Jacen drew his lightsaber, switched it on, and let it blaze into the darkness. Tenel Ka raised hers as well.

Jacen hoped his sister was all right, wherever she was . . . that she had managed to escape somehow, that she had found safety with Lowie.

Lowie!

Jacen looked up into the starlit sky.

Tenel Ka straightened, suddenly alert again, and waved her lightsaber back and forth. "Do you sense it?" she asked.

"Yes," Jacen said. "The *Rock Dragon*. It's coming!"

It appeared at first as a shadow against the sky, droning as it cruised low over the mountains. Soon a constellation of running lights twinkled their message of warmth, of encouragement. The ship was searching for them.

Jacen jumped up and down, yelling, "Lowie, we're here! We're *here!*"

Tenel Ka stood tall beside him and whirled her turquoise blade overhead.

The *Rock Dragon* wavered for a moment, then altered its course and arrowed straight toward them. "He's seen us!" Jacen exclaimed.

Tenel Ka shook the old Twi'lek exile. "Kur, we are saved. You must come with us."

"No . . . take me to the Bright Lands," he gasped.

The *Rock Dragon* hovered, seeking a place to land, but found no clear patch on the broken, rocky ridge.

"You can always choose the Bright Lands later," Jacen said, hope lending strength to his voice. "But for now, why not *help* the Twi'lek people? Nolaa Tarkona has done terrible things to them. Maybe you could help set everything right again."

As the *Rock Dragon* hovered in the air, buffeted by freezing winds, its ramp extended until it nearly touched the mountaintop. Kur didn't struggle or argue as they lifted him onto the ramp and carried him through the hatch.

Inside the bright cockpit, Lowie and Sirra both howled a greeting. Their fur bristled and their fangs flashed with exultation.

Jacen and Tenel Ka, still shivering, sank gratefully to the floor. The deck plates were so warm and welcoming that Jacen could think of no place he would rather have been.

He just wished his sister were there with him.

21

WITH A SUDDEN uneasy tingle felt through the Force, Jaina detected the danger before her eyes could spot anything outside in the unrelenting glare of day. She stood in the shadow of the alcove she had excavated, letting her eyes adjust.

Grabbing Raynar by the shoulder, she looked at the washed-out landscape under the pummeling sunlight. "They're coming," she said.

Raynar's eyes closed in their dim hiding place. His shoulders slumped, and he panted heavily, dragging in breaths of too-hot air that seemed to scorch the lining of his lungs. "Then we'd better get ready to fight."

Jaina gripped her lightsaber. The handle felt hot against her blistered palm. Raynar, without a Jedi weapon of his own, picked up a chunk of the rock Jaina had sliced free to create their cave. He hefted it in his hand, ready to throw.

Reaching out with her Jedi senses, Jaina could

tell that their stalkers were coming closer, closer. She could sense their anger, their hatred of humans. . . .

Raynar's eyes opened wide. "It's Hovrak!"

Jaina pressed her back against the wall, felt the heat throb against her skin. She did not switch on her lightsaber blade. They would remain in the darkness; it might gain them an additional second of surprise.

The heat-suited soldiers, though, made no attempt at stealth. When they discovered the freshly hewn cleft in the rock, one of the guards shouted in triumph. He stumbled forward in his unwieldy silver suit. Swinging his blaster from left to right, he stepped into the opening, prepared to fire—but Jaina was ready for him.

In a single blurred movement she switched on her lightsaber and slashed. The Jedi blade severed the business end of the blaster, leaving only a smoldering lump.

Then Raynar threw his rock with Force-enhanced power, hitting the guard hard in the stomach and knocking him backward toward the rocky ledge. His gloved hands clawed at the rocks, trying to catch his balance, but to no avail. The jagged edges ripped open his suit, and the guard's wail echoed inside his reflective helmet as he toppled over the side.

Hovrak called the rest of his team to a halt, shouting for them to retreat to the side of the ledge. Then, targeting on Jaina's glowing lightsaber, the guards fired into the grotto shadows, from a protected position.

Trapped like a womp rat in a box canyon, Jaina swung her lightsaber to deflect the blaster bolts. Raynar crouched at the back of the crevice to keep out of the way, hurling an occasional rock at their unseen enemies. Jaina clenched her jaw and fought with all of her Jedi skills, not daring to trust her dazzled eyes on the heat-washed ledge.

The silver-suited guards fired repeatedly. "Shall we set to stun?" one of them said.

"No, just kill her," Hovrak said. "And the other one too."

One of the three remaining guards blasted away at the mass of solid rock overhanging the crevice entrance. After volley upon volley, the overhang began to glow red with the heat it had absorbed.

Hovrak growled in anticipation. "Keep firing! They have no defense against us."

When Jaina stepped forward to deflect the new volley of fire, Raynar popped out of his shadowy shelter. He hefted another sharp-edged rock, then hurled it with perfect aim, so that it struck Hovrak's faceplate and cracked the reflectorized transparisteel. Raynar ducked back into hiding as the wolfman roared, stumbled backward, and barely regained his balance on the ledge.

One of the guards focused on Jaina and fired, ignoring the other activity around him. She deflected the shot, using her dazzling blade to knock the blaster bolt back to its source. The energy bolt caught the guard full in the chest and left a smoking hole in his reflective suit. Mortally wounded, the guard gasped and gargled, then slumped off the fiery cliffside.

Hovrak now had only two guards remaining.

"You'll need more help than this to defeat a Jedi Knight," Jaina shouted defiantly. Her throat burned; her cracked lips were bleeding; crusty salt from evaporated perspiration sparkled on her skin—but she was entirely focused on the battle now, flowing with the Force.

Hovrak snarled, uncomfortable now that his faceplate was broken. The outside air felt too hot to breathe, despite the suit's laboring air-conditioning units. "Soon we won't need to worry about humans ever again," he taunted them. "When the Diversity Alliance gets hold of the Emperor's plague, every one of you will die, from one end of the galaxy to the other."

"*You'll* die first," Jaina shouted back, stifling her horror at the plan Hovrak had just revealed. Now she knew what Nolaa Tarkona had intended all along.

Raynar threw rock after sharp rock at Hovrak and the guards. They stopped trying to melt the overhang and turned their blaster fire at him, but Raynar dodged away, drawing agility from the Force.

In frustration, the last two guards fired again. With no place to run, Jaina and Raynar stood at the edge of the narrow path, far from the temperate zone in the mountains where Lowie had planned to rescue them. On every side, sharp black boulders blocked any hope of escape.

Jaina stepped slightly in front of Raynar. She was willing to fight to the death. She saw no other choice. . . .

The *Lightning Rod* shot out of hyperspace, emerging as close to Ryloth's gravity well as Zekk's daring calculations would allow. Luke Skywalker sat in the copilot's seat, glad to be along on this rescue mission.

The ship streaked toward the atmosphere like a comet, broadcasting the access code Lusa had supplied, but not bothering to pause or request clearance to approach the planet. Zekk hoped his bold rush would get him past any sentinels that patrolled the orbital lanes around the Twi'lek homeworld.

"It's hard coming back here," Lusa said, trying to maintain her balance on all four hooves as the ship rolled from side to side. "Nolaa Tarkona knows I betrayed her. The Diversity Alliance won't hesitate to kill me."

"Then we won't give them the chance," Zekk said grimly.

"She's already sent an assassin to kill you on Yavin 4, and he failed," Master Skywalker pointed out, looking at the centaur girl with understanding. "Sometimes we have to face our fears."

"My fears keep coming after me," Lusa said. "And now they're trying to hurt my friends."

Zekk dodged and rolled, pirouetting experimentally in space. Then, satisfied that the *Lightning Rod* was ready, he dove toward the mountain range at the terminator between day and night. "Let's just hope we make it down there without running into much resistance," he said, and powered up his weapons systems.

Two sentry cruisers homed in on the rapidly approaching intruder. Zekk recognized a Hornet Interceptor and a stripped-down Lancer frigate emblazoned with alien language glyphs. "Unidentified ship, you are trespassing in airspace held by the Diversity Alliance. You are not welcome in this system. If you do not depart immediately, you will be destroyed."

"Yeah, right," Zekk muttered. "Try me." Alarms sounded on his control panel, but he ignored them. Without acknowledging, he raced straight at the sentry ships and opened fire.

"They aren't prepared for any resistance yet," Luke said, his eyes half closed in concentration. "Their minds are too . . . complacent."

The sentry cruisers began to activate their weapons systems and power up their shields. Suddenly aware of their danger, both craft spun out of the way and arched upward, but not before the *Lightning Rod*'s rapid, low-power blaster bolts scored some important hits.

"Hah! Right in the sensors," Zekk crowed. He

clapped his hands in triumph. "They're blind now until they can reset their systems."

"Leave them, then," Luke said. "We need to hurry. I sense that Jacen and Jaina are in trouble."

Lusa braced herself. The *Lightning Rod* scraped into the atmosphere while the two Diversity Alliance sentry vessels spun about. Disoriented in space, the two ships drifted so close to each other that they nearly collided before their respective commanders regained control.

Zekk roared down to cloud level, where huge tornadolike heat storms spawned by the temperature discontinuity between the frigid night side and the hot day side buffeted the ship. The wind currents knocked the *Lightning Rod* back and forth, but Lusa knew where they had to go. With terse accuracy, she directed Zekk toward the section of mountain range that held the tunnels controlled by Nolaa Tarkona.

"I spent plenty of time there," Lusa said, her crystalline horns glimmering. The muscles in her back rippled as she paced the deck and snorted uneasily. "I never thought I'd go back willingly. But this is for my friends."

"That's why it's an important step in your healing process," Master Skywalker said.

Lusa nodded. "For my friends . . . ," she repeated.

"Hang on," Zekk said. "I'm increasing speed. Those sentry cruisers are trying to sound an alarm." The *Lightning Rod* soared straight along the day side slopes of the mountain range.

On the open channel Zekk heard a strident warning being transmitted now that one of the ships had managed to get its main generators back on-line—but no one responded. Perhaps the Diversity Alliance was already too busy with its own emergencies.

Lusa pressed her face against the sloped transparisteel of the cockpit windows. "Look—down there on the mountainside!" she said. "What are those lights?"

Zekk frowned and studied the area the centaur girl had pointed to. "Looks like blaster fire."

"And a lightsaber," Master Skywalker added. "Somebody's fighting down there."

"It's Jaina!" Zekk said with absolute certainty. "Hold on down there, we're on our way!"

Though normally reluctant to use his Jedi senses, Zekk let the Force tingle through him. It made him self-conscious to use the Force, here in the presence of the Jedi Master, but Zekk knew he was doing the right thing.

The *Lightning Rod,* its laser cannons powered up to full charge, swooped to the rescue.

"Jaina is sure going to be surprised," he said.

The glaring sun and bright blaster fire had nearly blinded Jaina. She could hardly see anything other than her own lightsaber. Her arms were so weary she could barely raise them, but she sidestepped, deflected, struck. She could not allow herself to slow down. Hovrak had only two henchmen left. She and Raynar still had a chance, though it was a slim one.

Jaina took little note of any sound beyond the exploding blasters, the hum of her lightsaber, and the snarl of the Adjutant Advisor. The roaring that built louder and louder in the air simply did not register. She continued to fight, trying not to think ahead . . . though she did feel an unexpected surge of hope through the Force.

"It's a ship! There's a ship coming!" Raynar exclaimed.

Hovrak and his two guards looked up just in time to see the *Lightning Rod* streak toward the cliff opening. With pinpoint accuracy, the ship fired. Both guards were blasted off the rockface in the surprise attack. Hovrak stumbled back, flailing in the air. A section of the cliff wall melted behind him. Jaina and Raynar pressed themselves back into the crevice as cherry-red rocks fell smoking and steaming down into the chasm below. Hovrak managed to throw himself against an outcropping and hold on, roaring in outrage through his cracked helmet.

As the ship hovered in front of the embattled alcove, the cargo door of the *Lightning Rod* hissed open. Zekk grinned. "I thought it was supposed to be your turn to rescue me this time, Jaina. Need a lift?"

Luke Skywalker sat in the pilot's seat. "Jaina! Raynar! Jump in."

Lusa raced to the cargo bay and held out her

hands. Jaina pushed Raynar up onto the unsteady ramp; the young man winced as he touched the hot metal, but he hauled himself aboard. Jostled by wind currents, the *Lightning Rod* hovered near the cliff above the blasted chasm.

"Your turn, Jaina!" Zekk said, helping Raynar inside. "We're just about ready!" He gestured to Master Skywalker at the pilot's controls.

Seeing Raynar safe, Jaina clipped her lightsaber to her side. Then she jumped. Once on the ramp, she fell to her knees and pulled herself along. "I'm on," she shouted.

Back in the cockpit, Zekk and Master Skywalker began to move the *Lightning Rod*. But at the last second, Hovrak bunched his muscles and leaped across the widening gap. With one silver-gloved hand he grabbed the piston support of the *Lightning Rod*'s ramp; with his other, he clutched Jaina's foot. "You can't escape!" he roared.

"Yes we will," Jaina said, struggling against him.

Lusa leaned over, extending her arms to Jaina.

Hovrak glanced up, his wolf eyes slitted. "Lusa! *Another* traitor!"

"No. I'm no longer deluded," Lusa said. "That doesn't make me a traitor—it just makes me a bit smarter than you."

Hovrak strained to haul himself aboard the ship as it soared higher into the air . . . though what the wolfman intended to do, Jaina couldn't guess. She thrashed and kicked at him, but he would not let go of her foot.

Her skin burned. Her hands were raw from where blisters had popped open. Luke took the *Lightning Rod* high into the air, away from the rocky uplift, out into the hotter skies of Ryloth.

"You'd better get inside!" Zekk called back to Jaina. The wind howled through the opening, rippling their clothes. "Stop playing around back there."

"Who's playing?" Jaina said, kicking once again at Hovrak. Her foot struck his helmet, cracking the transparisteel plate all the way open.

The Adjutant Advisor clung tenaciously to her leg. He held on with both hands, more intent on dragging her down with him than in getting to relative safety aboard the ship.

Jaina's knees slipped on the metal ramp. She scrambled for purchase, but Hovrak's weight dragged her back down the ramp toward the opening and the long drop. Hot winds from the canyon roared in through the opening. Raynar pulled himself to his hands and knees in the cargo bay. He slapped the control switch for the ramp, closing it halfway so that Jaina could climb in. Hovrak's feet dangled over the edge.

Seizing the opportunity, Hovrak finally hauled himself aboard. He released his vicious grip on Jaina with a triumphant glare in his bloodshot animal eyes.

"Lusa, do something!" Raynar yelled.

But the centaur girl was already taking action. As Hovrak stood up, Lusa reared and kicked him full in the chest, knocking him back onto the ramp. Raynar punched the controls again. The ramp opened wide.

The *Lightning Rod* soared over a lava-filled crevice. Hovrak, in his slippery suit, slid back down and out into open air. The plummeting wolfman flailed. His protective suit glittered as he dropped for thousands of meters . . . until he plunged with a puff of bright yellow flame into a sluggish river of molten rock. The lava bubbled and swallowed up the dark stain. In a heartbeat, nothing remained of Hovrak.

Panting and distraught, Jaina crawled farther into the cargo area, and the *Lightning Rod*'s ramp finally hissed shut. Jaina took a deep breath of blessedly cool air and then fell trembling next to Raynar.

The two were battered, sunburned, grime-encrusted messes, but she grinned at the young man from Alderaan, then offered a weak wave to Luke and Zekk in the cockpit.

"How can I help?" the centaur girl asked.

"We could both use a drink right about now," Jaina gasped.

Raynar looked gratefully up at Lusa. "Cold water?"

"Make it a double," Jaina added.

22

TOGETHER, THE *LIGHTNING Rod* and the *Rock Dragon* sped upward out of Ryloth's atmosphere. As they flew, pursued now by Diversity Alliance ships, Zekk gained new admiration for Luke Skywalker. Even in an old-fashioned freighter like the *Lightning Rod,* the Jedi Master's training as a fighter pilot was obvious.

Zekk was glad to witness the legendary skill of the X-wing pilot who had destroyed the first Death Star. Master Skywalker maneuvered the ship, expertly dodging quadlaser fire from their disorganized pursuers, while Zekk answered each attack with a volley of fire from the *Lightning Rod*'s weapons systems.

Zekk longed to leave the weapons controls to tend to Jaina's injuries and reassure himself that she was all right. But that would have to wait until they got away from the Diversity Alliance.

"Hang on back there, we're not out of this yet," Zekk said. He tossed Lusa the *Lightning Rod*'s emergency medkit. The centaur girl was more than competent enough to care for the two patients until they could get to a real medical center.

Luke threw the *Lightning Rod* into a sideways spin just moments before laser cannon fire exploded behind them.

Beside them, the *Rock Dragon* pulled into a sharp loop and arced backward. Seconds later, Zekk saw explosions to the stern of the *Lightning Rod* on his viewscreens.

A loud Wookiee bellow and a triumphant warble blasted from the comm system's speakers. Em Teedee's exclamation followed. "Oh, well done, Master Lowbacca, Mistress Sirrakuk!"

Zekk scanned the space around them for Diversity Alliance ships. "We're all clear!"

Luke nodded. "Thanks for the assistance, *Rock Dragon*," he said. "We've got Raynar and Jaina. Are the others with you?"

"Oh, yes, Master Luke. And more," Em Teedee replied. "Master Jacen and Mistress Tenel Ka have brought along a guest—a Twi'lek gentleman. They assure us he's a friend . . . or at least he is no friend of Nolaa Tarkona's."

Luke's eyebrows raised in surprise. "A Twi'lek? I'll have to trust their judgment on that. Anyway, it's about time we got this team back together."

A pair of jubilant Wookiee voices roared their agreement.

"I heartily concur, Master Luke," Em Teedee said. In the background, Lowie barked a question. "Master Lowbacca wishes to inquire whether we should all rendezvous at Yavin 4?"

Zekk cast a worried glance back at Jaina and Raynar, assessing their injuries.

Lusa shook her head. "I'm not sure the jungle moon is a good idea. We're going to need some full-fledged bacta tanks, I think."

"Where we're going, they've got some of the best," Master Skywalker said. He leaned forward and spoke into the comm again. "Negative, Lowie. Sirra, Em Teedee, set your course for Coruscant. We'll meet you on the private landing pad at the Imperial Palace."

The reunion of the young Jedi Knights on Coruscant was joyous. But Jacen sensed that for Lowie, the triumph of their escape was bittersweet—since Raaba had remained with the Diversity Alliance.

Han, Leia, and Anakin Solo welcomed family and friends with a mixture of horror, relief, and reproach. They had a great many concerns, and Leia vowed to bring the full resources of the New Republic into play. Lowie, Sirra, and Lusa spent a good deal of time in deep conversation with Master Skywalker, Chewbacca, Han, and Leia, sharing what they had learned from the Diversity Alliance.

Jaina and Raynar, Jacen and Tenel Ka were hustled off to the medical center adjacent to the

Imperial Palace. Now that the urgency of escape was behind them, healing the wounded took priority. The young Jedi Knights finally had a chance to feel the full force of the damage their bodies had sustained. Zekk rarely left Jaina's side.

Despite their various injuries, all of the young friends were reminded several times by their Jedi Master and the leader of the New Republic that their actions, though brave, had also been very foolish.

When Tenel Ka's grandmother arrived unexpectedly, however, she did not reproach her granddaughter. No one had sent the former queen word of Tenel Ka's injuries or that she was being taken to Coruscant. Yet somehow she had known, and Jacen sensed that Ta'a Chume was secretly quite proud of what Tenel Ka had done.

Han and Leia, though proud of their children, still chided them hours after Jacen and Jaina's return. Finally, Jaina had had enough of her parents' censure. "But if we hadn't gone to Ryloth," she blurted out, "we'd never have learned that the Diversity Alliance was secretly plotting to wipe out all humans!"

Seeing the stricken look on his mother's face, Jacen had the grace to feel ashamed for the turmoil they had put her through. He could well imagine how worried she must have been. "We're sorry we didn't trust you enough to tell you what we were doing, Mom," he said as gently as he could. "But now we've told you everything we know, and there's *no one* we trust more to decide where we go from here."

His mother gave Jacen a grateful smile. "The Twi'lek you brought back with you—Kur—has been very helpful," she said. "We've also learned a few things about the Diversity Alliance."

"From the Bothan who tried to kill me?" Lusa said.

The Chief of State nodded. "I think the next step is to present what we've found out in a meeting of the New Republic Senate. So concentrate on getting well. Into the bacta tanks with all of you. I'm going to need your help when you're a little stronger."

Jacen looked around at his sister, Tenel Ka, Zekk, Raynar, and Lowie, who had Em Teedee clipped to his belt and Sirra close beside him. "We're already stronger," he said. "Now that we're together again." Lowie roared his support.

"Uncle Luke has always said we're stronger together," Jaina agreed.

"This is a fact," Tenel Ka said.

The best-selling saga continues . . .

The Emperor's Plague

Bornan Thul's secret is out: he's been protecting a deadly plague that could devastate the galaxy if released. And the evil Nolaa Tarkona—leader of the Diversity Alliance—knows where it is hidden.

Now Jacen, Jaina, and their allies must race against time. As a massive battle rages between New Republic soldiers and the forces of the Diversity Alliance, the young Jedi Knights must find and destroy the plague before it can be released.

But they first must face Nolaa Tarkona. And her very lethal hired hand, Boba Fett.

Turn the page for a special preview of the next book in the STAR WARS: YOUNG JEDI KNIGHTS series:

The Emperor's Plague

Coming in January from Boulevard Books!

Raynar still couldn't believe that his mother had risked coming out of hiding to see him on Coruscant. Now both he and Aryn Dro Thul stood on the highest balcony of the Bornaryn headquarters building, overlooking a broad plaza that bustled with people.

At the heart of the plaza, a fountain with hundreds of tiers burbled, trickled, gushed, and spouted. The spectacular display reminded him of the Dro family's Ceremony of the Waters. It seemed to him like years since his entire family had gathered together for the celebration.

For the millionth time since his father's disappearance, Raynar found himself wishing that his whole family could be together again, wishing that he had remembered to enjoy those times more in the past. . . .

"This view was one of the reasons Bornan and I chose this building for our headquarters." His mother wore her midnight-blue gown shot with silver and belted with a sash in the colors of the House of Thul. Her fingers toyed with the sash and her lips curved in a faint smile. "Somehow I feel closer to your father just standing here."

"He's in danger, you know," Raynar said.

Without looking away from the fountain, Aryn nodded. "Tell me what you've learned."

"It all started with the Twi'lek leader, Nolaa Tarkona. Dad was negotiating some trade agreements with her when he disappeared."

Gaze still fixed on the fountain, Aryn nodded. "Bornan was planning to meet with her at the Shumavar trade conference . . . but he never arrived."

"Well, Uncle Tyko was right about one thing. Dad wasn't kidnapped. He *decided* to disappear, but he had a good reason. Nolaa Tarkona had started an interplanetary political movement called the Diversity Alliance. It's supposed to bring nonhuman species together to right the wrongs of the past. Unfortunately, Nolaa Tarkona decided that the only way to right those wrongs was by destroying humans."

"But why should she have singled out Bornan?" Aryn asked.

"An alien scavenger named Fonterrat discovered an Imperial storehouse containing a plague that could kill humans quickly. Fonterrat offered to sell the information to Nolaa Tarkona, but he refused to deal directly with her. Instead he insisted that she send a neutral party to meet with him on the ancient planet Kuar."

"And so Nolaa Tarkona sent Bornan?" Aryn said.

"Right. As far as we know, Dad exchanged a time-locked case full of credits for a navicomputer that contained the location of the plague storehouse. Just a simple exchange. Dad was supposed to take the navicomputer to Nolaa Tarkona at the Shumavar conference. He would never even have known what he was carrying— but at the last minute I guess Fonterrat confessed it to him."

Still looking down at the bustling plaza far below, Aryn Dro Thul shook her head. "This plague sounds a little far-fetched. That scavenger could have been exaggerating."

"He wasn't," Raynar said. "The plague is real. Fonterrat had given Nolaa Tarkona at least one sample, and Nolaa used that sample to booby-trap his payment. At Fonterrat's next stop, an all-human colony called Gammalin, the plague killed everyone. The colonists locked up Fonterrat before the plague killed them, and he himself died in a tiny jail since no one was left alive to take care of him. Ever since then, Dad has been on the run, trying to keep the navicomputer away from Nolaa Tarkona. We can't let her get her hands on that plague, or the entire human race will be destroyed."

Aryn's shoulders dropped. "That sounds like your father—but why didn't he simply destroy the navicomputer, or bring the information here to Coruscant?"

"It's not that easy," Raynar said. "We know that some members of the Diversity Alliance have infiltrated the New Republic government. A Bothan soldier wearing a New Republic uniform even tried to kill Lusa on Yavin 4. Maybe Dad suspected the information wasn't safe if he delivered it here."

"Yes, your father always had good people instincts," Aryn agreed.

"Then he probably also guessed that Nolaa Tarkona would stop at nothing to get that plague, with or without the navicomputer. When Jacen, Jaina, Tenel Ka, and I were prisoners on Ryloth, we learned that she hopes to release that plague and infect every last human in the galaxy."

"I wish I were there to help your father," Aryn said.

"I wish I could help him too," Raynar said, taking his mother's hand a bit awkwardly. It felt strange at first, but he had come to realize in the past months how easy it was to lose the things and the people that you cared about. "I'm glad you're here, Mom," he said. "I didn't expect you to come out of hiding until we had found Dad."

Aryn Dro Thul stood tall, straightened her shoulders, and looked into Raynar's eyes. "Sometimes we simply have to face our worst fears," she said. "You've shown so much courage since your father disappeared. I'm very proud of you, you know."

Raynar sighed. "I guess facing our fears is a part of growing up."

His mother raised her eyebrows at him. "Maybe. Even so, it never gets any easier."

With a contented smile, Leia Organa Solo gazed slowly around the meal table in the Solo family's quarters of the Imperial Palace. It was still hard to believe that her husband and three children were here at home, all at the same time. She allowed herself to enjoy the moment, though it had taken a galactic crisis to bring them together.

"More nerf sausage, Master Jacen?" See-Threepio offered. "It is a particular Corellian favorite."

"Maybe just one," Jacen answered. Leia noted that Jacen was taller than she had remembered. It amazed her to see how the twins and Anakin grew and changed each time they returned from their studies at the Jedi academy.

After serving Jacen, the gold protocol droid turned to Jaina. She held her hands over her plate, as if to protect it from Threepio's enthusiastic service. "Couldn't eat another bite," Jaina protested.

"Over here, Goldenrod," Han said, holding out his plate for more. "These are just like the ones Dewlanna used to make for me."

Anakin said, "I have a feeling you're all going

to need your strength when you speak to the New Republic Senate tomorrow."

"Tomorrow?" the twins asked in unison.

Leia said, "I've scheduled a special meeting of the New Republic Senate for tomorrow morning. I'd like you and all of your friends there to present your findings. I think the whole galaxy needs to know what the Diversity Alliance has planned."

The New Republic senate chambers were full to overflowing. Jaina looked uncertainly through the door into the crowded room and then back at her mother. The Chief of State shrugged. "We had a vote coming up on several major issues, so I requested full attendance today. There are senators and delegates in there whom I haven't seen in months."

Jaina attempted a lopsided grin. "Must be something in the air, huh?" She glanced around at her assembled friends, all of whom were aware of how important their words would be.

Tenel Ka said, "Perhaps they heard of our intention to discuss the Diversity Alliance."

"More than likely," Leia admitted. "I know you all understand how much is at stake here."

"If you want, I could try to loosen up the crowd with a joke." Jacen waggled his eyebrows. Leia turned toward him with a startled look and opened her mouth as if to speak. "Hey, I was just kidding," Jacen said, holding up his hands in a placating gesture. Lowie rumbled deep in his throat. "Okay—bad timing, I admit. It's just that we all seem so tight and edgy."

"You're right," Jaina said, drawing a slow deep breath and letting the Force flow through her to relax her. A wave of calm clarity washed the worry from her mind. Around her, Lowie, Sirra, Tenel Ka, Zekk, Lusa, and Raynar were also using Jedi relaxation techniques. Her father and Chewbacca along with her uncle Luke, the Jedi historian Tionne, and Kur, the Twi'lek politician rescued from exile on Ryloth, had already taken their seats toward the front of the Senate chamber.

"Well then, what are we waiting for?" Jaina asked.

Much later, after they had told all their adventures and delivered their alarming news, it still wasn't over.

Jaina grew defensive as yet another representative stood up to take the floor. She could sense her brother's bafflement at the response with which the Senate had greeted their announcement. Tenel Ka, as usual, was stolid and alert, probably scanning the crowd for any signs of trouble.

Only Chief of State Leia Organa Solo seemed perfectly calm, as if the reactions of the senators and delegates were exactly what she had expected. She looked around the room with a practiced ease, seeing everything, listening to everything, gauging the reactions of her audience. Jaina bit her lower lip, willing herself to be more like her mother, ordering herself to listen to the squeaking Chadra Fan senator with an open mind.

"And so, it is not the people of the Diversity Alliance who should be censured. I suggest that these willful *human* children need to be taught true respect for legal governments," Senator Trubor concluded, triumphantly swiveling his triangular batlike ears.

Alarmed, Jaina looked over at her parents, or Luke Skywalker, hoping they would react to such accusations. But already it seemed too many humans had spoken out. Luke met Jaina's gaze, giving his silent support.

Without comment, her mother nodded and announced the name of the next speaker. "Senator J'mesk Iman."

The small cherub-faced Tamran steepled his fingers at chest level and bowed slightly. J'mesk Iman's expressive brows rose as he spoke. "Forgive me if I have misunderstood the situation, but—it is not the habit of the New Republic to meddle in the affairs of local governments, is it?"

"No," Leia said slowly, "it isn't."

"Then perhaps this could all be viewed as a cultural misunderstanding." J'mesk Iman spread his hands in a traditional gesture his people used when offering peace. "From an objective point of view, what these young Jedi did might be described as well-intentioned but ill-advised. There should be no need to consider it an outright act of espionage."

Jaina shifted uncomfortably at the ambassador's benign condemnation and waited to hear what else he might have to say.

"At worst, the venture may be described as a willful and unlawful act of aggressive intrusion against a legal sovereign government."

Jaina felt her brother flinch. She sensed rather than heard a growl forming deep in Lowie's throat; though the Wookiee restrained himself, she could see the black streak of fur over his eye bristling. Tenel Ka, on the other hand, listened with her usual stoicism, her thoughts impassive and unreadable, as if the Senate's mixed response was no surprise to her.

"Since the children's arrival was neither announced nor authorized—since it was, in fact, covert," Iman continued. "Both the Diversity Alliance and the government of Ryloth had ample reason to view it as an act of aggression."

"But we explained what we were doing there," Jacen objected. "They were holding Lowie against his will. And they still threw us into their spice mines."

Iman fixed them all with a serious look and cocked his head to one side. When he answered, though, his voice was not unkind. "Yet had any of you *requested* their government's permission to enter its headquarters?"

"No," Jaina answered truthfully. "But we never

intended any harm. We just wanted to get our friend back."

"Even so, since your mission was not a diplomatic one, and not sanctioned by any government, you placed yourselves under the jurisdiction of local laws by trespassing as you did. I do not believe even the New Republic could allow such an intrusion without punishing the perpetrators. It is only natural that any government should want to deter others from doing what you had done."

Jaina bit her lower lip. She knew there was no way to refuse the ambassador's words.

"But what about the spice mines?" Raynar asked.

"Very well, then. How long did you spend in the spice mines?" Iman asked.

"A few days," Jaina answered. "We didn't have chronometers with us."

"A harsh punishment perhaps for high-born youngsters such as yourselves," the alien senator said, "but not outside the realm of reason. Were you denied food or water or sleep?"

Jaina grimaced at the memory of the fungus they had been expected to eat and the foul-tasting water they had been offered, but she shook her head. Raynar took a sudden interest in studying the floor near his feet and said nothing. "But they never released us," Jaina pointed out. "Lowie had to help us escape."

The ambassador steepled his fingers at his chin and smiled. "And yet here you all are, alive and well. So allow me to summarize. You broke into the headquarters of a well-respected political movement. The legal government there sentenced you to a short term of unpleasant yet lenient punishment—long enough for you to learn a valuable lesson, we can hope. Then, before you had served your complete term, your friends—who at the time were *working* for the Diversity Alliance," at this, Iman's brows rose expressively, "released you from captivity and assisted you in departing Ryloth without further punishment. And during all that time, the only true injuries you sustained were a result of the ill-advised paths you chose when leaving."

Jaina drew in a deep breath and let it out slowly. It wasn't fair when the story was presented that way.

At this point Lowie spoke up in a series of rumbles, barks and growls. Em Teedee made a throat clearing sound to be sure he had the attention of the entire assembly and then provided a translation. "Master Lowbacca does not choose to dispute your interpretation of events surrounding the arrival and departure of his colleagues from Ryloth. He does, however, wish to clarify two facts. First: the current government on Ryloth does not necessarily represent the Twi'lek people"—at this point, the overthrown leader Kur stepped forward and nodded his confirmation—"And second: during their time working for the Diversity Alliance, Master Lowbacca, Mistress Sirrakuk, and Mistress Lusa all noted a distinct antihuman sentiment that had the distinct potential for expressing itself with some violence."

A stern looking centaur woman with glossy dark flanks and a long salt-and-pepper mane approached the floor. J'mesk Iman yielded his position, and Leia announced the new ambassador with a sense of relief. "Ambassador Suras Tonee, please speak."

Suras nodded to Leia and shook back her long dark mane. "I do not believe that any government is sacred. It may well be, as my colleague has said, that nothing more happened on Ryloth than a juvenile infraction of governmental laws and the punishment of that infraction." A murmur of approval ran through the Senate.

"*However,*" she continued, "if the government of Ryloth and the Diversity Alliance are stable and peaceful and do no more than work in the interests of their members, then they should have no objection to a simple diplomatic inspection. This would, of course, be prearranged and approved through appropriate channels with their government. Some of the charges against the Diversity Alliance are indeed troubling and warrant our attention. Therefore, I propose a simple fact-finding mission.

"The delegation should consist of a representative mixture of species and include a few members who are familiar with the government of Ryloth," she nodded to the Twi'lek Kur, "and the Diversity Alliance." Here she nodded to the

Wookiees and Lusa. "If we find no evidence of wrongdoing, as many of my colleagues expect, then this inspection will be the simplest method of putting the matter to rest."

From the corner of her eye Jaina saw her mother relax considerably. Taking a cue from her, Jaina ordered her muscles to unknot themselves. Ambassador D'Jeel approached the floor again, but from the small smile of triumph on her mother's face, Jaina knew that there was no longer any doubt of the outcome: a team of investigators would soon be on its way to Ryloth.

Then they would all find clear evidence of Nolaa Tarkona's schemes.

STAR WARS
YOUNG JEDI KNIGHTS

SHARDS OF ALDERAAN

Jacen and Jaina set off for the Alderaan system, determined to salvage a piece of the shattered planet as a gift for their mother. But amid the ghosts of a dead world, the twins are in for a lethal surprise: some ghosts still live. A long-lost enemy of the Solo family is about to return...

__1-57297-207-6/$5.99

DIVERSITY ALLIANCE

Everyone is searching for Bornan Thul. Not only is he father to one of Jacen and Jaina's fellow students, he holds the key to a secret coalition gaining power in the New Republic.

__1-57297-234-3/$5.99

Kevin J. Anderson and Rebecca Moesta

®, ™, & © 1997 Lucasfilm Ltd. All rights reserved.
Used Under Authorization